The Press Of People Opened For An Instant, Long Enough For Guy To Catch A Tantalizing Glimpse.

He blinked.

It couldn't be.

The crowd shifted again. *It was.* His gaze homed in on an achingly familiar blond head and a petite curvy feminine body that should've been nine hundred miles away in California.

His twin bent courteously to hear what the blonde was saying, and Guy's eyes narrowed dangerously when her slim hand pushed a pair of designer sunglasses to the top of her head. The action revealed the curve of a cheek he'd stroked with his fingertips under the cover of darkness, the corner of a lush, smiling mouth he'd kissed until all smiling had ceased and she'd moaned instead.

God, he remembered those moans....

Little mewing sounds that made him go wild with hunger.

So what the hell was Avery Lancaster doing here?

Dear Reader,

For me one of the greatest thrills of writing is the research I get to do for every new book…entering an unknown world and claiming it for my hero and heroine. What I learn about the world they live in helps me to shape the people they are.

Usually writing—and researching—is a solitary experience.

So it was a lot of fun to be able to compare pictures, notes and snippets of information and history about Aspen with six other writers as the Jarrods became real to all of us. There were lots of oohs and aahs—and plenty of ideas sparked. Maureen found the perfect Jarrod Manor, Emilie Rose discovered an old silver mine, Maxine Sullivan dreamed up a handsome doctor who I'm sure will have his own romance soon, Heidi Betts planned the most wonderful Christmas wedding and Kathie DeNosky created a spa so sinfully luxurious I want to visit it!

It was fabulous working with Maureen Child, Kathie DeNosky, Maxine Sullivan, Emilie Rose and Heidi Betts on DYNASTIES: THE JARRODS.

I hope you enjoy the series as much as we enjoyed writing it. Please feel free to write me at tessa@tessaradley.com and let me know what you think.

Happy reading,

Tessa

TESSA RADLEY

FALLING FOR HIS PROPER MISTRESS

Silhouette
Desire

Published by Silhouette Books

America's Publisher of Contemporary Romance

Special thanks and acknowledgment to Tessa Radley
for her contribution to the
DYNASTIES: THE JARRODS miniseries.
For my cousin Merope

The only person I know who can find a restaurant
where sinfully rich chocolate cake is served first on the menu
and entrées appear on the dessert menu described as
something to fill the space left over!

SILHOUETTE BOOKS

PLEASE RECYCLE
THIS PRODUCT IS RECYCLABLE

ISBN-13: 978-0-373-73043-8

Recycling programs
for this product may
not exist in your area.

FALLING FOR HIS PROPER MISTRESS

Visit Silhouette Books at www.eHarlequin.com

Printed in U.S.A.

Books by Tessa Radley

Silhouette Desire

Black Widow Bride #1794
Rich Man's Revenge #1806
*The Kyriakos Virgin Bride #1822
*The Apollonides Mistress Scandal #1829
*The Desert Bride of Al Sayed #1835
Pride & a Pregnancy Secret #1849
†Mistaken Mistress #1901
†Spaniard's Seduction #1907
†Pregnancy Proposal #1914
†The Untamed Sheik #1933
Billion-Dollar Baby Bargain #1961
Millionaire Under the Mistletoe #1985
Falling for His Proper Mistress #2030

*Billionaire Heirs
†The Saxon Brides

TESSA RADLEY

loves traveling, reading and watching the world around her. As a teen Tessa wanted to be an intrepid foreign correspondent. But after completing a bachelor of arts degree and marrying her sweetheart, she became fascinated by law and ended up studying further and practicing as an attorney in a city firm.

A six-month break traveling through Australia with her family reawoke the yen to write. And life as a writer suits her perfectly—traveling and reading count as research, and as for analyzing the world…well, she can think "what if?" all day long. When she's not reading, traveling or thinking about writing she's spending time with her husband, her two sons or her zany and wonderful friends. You can contact Tessa through her Web site, www.tessaradley.com.

From The Last Will And Testament Of Don Jarrod

…and to my son, **Guy,** I leave ten acres of private land. They compose the meadow, just beyond Willow Lodge. The view overlooks Roaring Fork. It was here that I often came to contemplate life and the choices I had made. Some I have regretted, others I have gladly lived with. It is my hope that you will build a home on this land, a place you will feel is truly your home. And if you are as lucky as I was, you'll build that home with someone you deeply love. Make the right decisions in your life, my son, and happiness will find you.

One

Everything was running smoothly.

Well, almost everything, Guy Jarrod amended as he strode into the cobbled square that lay at the heart of Aspen's famous Jarrod Ridge resort.

Erica Prentice, his newly discovered half sister, had sprung the unwelcome news on the family at breakfast this morning that Art Lloyd, one of the Food and Wine Gala speakers, had called yesterday to cancel his appearance because of a bad bout of influenza. Apart from the minor headache of finding someone to replace Art, the annual festival was on track and the tall, snowy-white marquees that lined the square on three sides hummed with activity.

If his old man had been here, even he would've admitted that the spectacle was impressive.

Heaviness pressed down on Guy's heart. Don Jarrod, his father—and an Aspen legend—was gone. Forever. Yet Jarrod Ridge remained a monument to his father's life's work.

A large shadow floated over Guy. Squinting skyward, he saw awestruck faces peering down at him from baskets that hung below brightly hued balloons drifting lazily across the morning sky. Guy's mood lifted and he raised a hand to wave before making for the nearest marquee that, even this early in the day, was already crowded.

He could see Erica huddled next to Gavin, one of his two younger brothers, her finger stabbing the air as she emphasized a point. And over to the right, beside the wine-tasting tent where an early-bird charity auction was already happening, his twin brother, Blake, was talking to—

The press of people opened for an instant, long enough for Guy to catch a tantalizing glimpse.

He blinked.

It couldn't be.

The crowd shifted again.

It was.

His gaze homed in on an achingly familiar blond head and a petite curvy feminine body that should've been nine hundred miles away in California.

His twin bent courteously to hear what the blonde was saying, and Guy's eyes narrowed dangerously when her slim hand pushed a pair of designer sunglasses to the top of her head. The action revealed the curve of a cheek he'd stroked with his fingertips under the cover of darkness, the corner of a lush, smiling mouth he'd kissed until all smiling had ceased and she'd moaned instead.

God, he remembered those moans….

Little mewing sounds that had clawed at his groin and made him go wild with hunger.

So what the hell was Avery Lancaster doing staring up at his twin in that intent fashion?

Without conscious thought, Guy began to move, long

strides that ate up the ground. All too soon he was looming over the Barbie-blonde who barely reached his shoulder.

She must have sensed his approach. It took only one startled glance from those wide china-blue eyes for Guy to feel the imperceptible tightening of his skin, the rippling of the muscles below. A slight shudder quaked through him before he remembered to breathe and sucked in a lungful of air. Being this close to Avery had always made him feel invincible, like some kind of superhero.

Not anymore.

Yet, for once, Avery looked rattled, too.

"Guy!"

In the month and a half—okay, so he'd kept count—*forty-nine days*—since he'd last seen her, Avery's sorcery hadn't diminished a whit. In her absence, Guy had half convinced himself he'd imagined it. No woman had that much power.

But standing beside her brought home that he hadn't imagined a thing. A once-over showed that her composure was back—if indeed it had ever slipped. Avery looked like she'd stepped from the pages of a glossy magazine that would have every female reader rushing to buy the floral dress she wore. Her soft honey-gold skin tempted his touch. Only the blond tendrils that had escaped the restraining sunglasses broke the model-like perfection and made her look tousled— and very, very kissable.

"Avery," he responded with just enough frost to cause Blake to raise an eyebrow.

"You two know each other?"

"Avery helped me review the wine list at Baratin."

His glare dared her to contradict him. Avery's gaze fell beneath the force of his—as he'd known it would. Traitor. It felt like a lifetime since the day she'd swept into his life with the force of a hurricane—and proved to be every bit as destructive. In reality little more than two months had passed since the day they'd met. Fourteen hours after that first meeting she'd been in his bed. The next day she'd moved out of the hotel where she'd been staying into his apartment. Two weeks later she'd been gone.

Yet instead of boasting about what a fabulous job she'd done at Baratin, Avery now turned her head away, presenting him with a smooth, flawlessly tanned cheek, and fixed her attention firmly back on Blake.

Over my dead body.

Guy's lips tightened. She could forget about seducing his brother. One Jarrod would have to be enough.

Blake grinned. "I remember you mentioning employing a freelance sommelier—you didn't tell me she was gorgeous."

Avery hadn't spared Guy another glance—he might as well have been invisible. And his normally brisk-and-businesslike twin hadn't taken his eyes off Avery. Irritation spiked through Guy as a rosy flush spread over her cheeks.

Could she have faked that?

A dimple appeared beside her mouth, and a little husky laugh followed. "Flatterer," she said to Blake, her polished fingertips fluttering like butterfly wings against his brother's arm.

Guy started to frown.

She'd better damn well stop flirting with Blake or he'd drag her away and send her packing back to Napa Valley. He wasn't having destruction follow in her wake as it had before.

He was onto Avery Lancaster.

She chose that moment to remove her hand from Blake's arm and flick the bangs off her forehead. The crossover neckline of the dress printed with pink roses—without a warning thorn in sight—pulled tight. Guy's lip curled. No magical illusion there, just plain feminine wiles, as old as Eve.

It infuriated Guy that even he wasn't immune. Giving himself a mental shake, he forced his eyes away from temptation, only to discover his charismatic twin still assessing her with amused interest.

Damn.

"You two must be brothers." The breathy voice that had once made him shiver with longing held a note of discovery.

Guy suppressed an annoyed growl as Blake instantly responded, "Guy is my twin."

"I knew there was something familiar about you—"

"Fraternal twins," Guy bit out, determined to make Avery stop examining Blake as if he was a juicy cut of filet mignon. "Not identical."

The gaze that switched to meet his with startling directness was carefully blank. "Funny, I didn't even know you had a brother, much less a twin," she murmured. "Or that you were one of the Aspen Jarrods."

Funny? They'd had an affair. Passionate. Explosive. Nothing remotely funny about it. Then she'd walked away. There'd been no obligation to bare his soul, dammit.

"Now you know—and, since you're obviously interested, I have two more brothers as well." Gavin and Trevor were every bit as eligible as Blake.

Despite the curve of her lips, her vivid blue eyes had dimmed, and held none of the sparkle he remembered. Only an unfamiliar wariness.

She should be worried.

Unless she was a fool. And, despite the sexy-Barbie exterior, Avery had never been dumb. In truth, the way it had played out *he'd* been the dumbass; *she'd* played him for the fool.

Guy snorted at how he'd fought a primal, gut-deep fear and tried to do romance. For her. How he'd planned the most romantic birthday gift he could dream up. An extravagant meal of all the foods he'd learned Avery loved. Shrimp tempura. A light salad with walnuts, blue cheese, pear and a hint of ginger. Cherries. Tiramisu. Baratin's frenetic Friday night bustle had been replaced with the intimacy of soft candlelight. Twenty-seven white candles—to match her birthday—glowed around one solitary table, with all the other chairs and tables packed away.

Surrounded by the aroma of the fluffy rolls he'd baked himself and the fragrance of cut flowers in tall vases filling the air, Guy had waited.

And waited…

And while he waited, his heart more exposed than he'd ever allowed, Avery had been seducing Jeffrey Morse.

The big romantic gesture had cost Guy more than a night's takings. It had cost him a week's sleep and most of his self-respect. And nearly two months later his pride still smarted.

Of course, if Avery had known he was one of the Jarrods from Jarrod Ridge, Aspen, Guy doubted she would have switched her attentions to Jeff, his Go Green business partner, so readily—despite Jeff's sizeable trust fund.

But the subject of his family had simply never come up. There hadn't been time. They'd either been talking about wine and work—or tumbling into bed. And Guy was suddenly, savagely glad that she hadn't known before he'd gotten a chance to discover exactly what she was.

Gold digger.

Well, there'd be no Jarrod gold for her here.…

Forcing himself to ignore her considerable physical endowments, he speared her with a cold stare. "What are you doing at Jarrod Ridge?"

The instant he bit out the words Guy wished he'd kept his mouth shut. What the hell did he care why she was here? He despised her. It was obvious that she'd come to Jarrod Ridge to prospect for another wealthy fool at a festival renowned for attracting the rich and famous. Jeff had sent her packing once guilt at the way he'd betrayed a friend had set in. Guy knew he should be grateful for his own lucky escape, that he'd found out Avery was looking for nothing more than a wealthy man.

Except gratitude was not the emotion that filled him as Avery's pink tongue slid across her pouty kiss-me-senseless bottom lip. In another woman the gesture might have suggested anxiety; in Avery it was pure feminine seduction. Her tongue retreated and Guy breathed again. Then her lush lips parted. Guy couldn't have glanced away if there'd been a gun against his head. Right now all he cared about was sexy Avery and her provocative, pink mouth.

Clenching his fists at his sides, Guy swore a silent streak.

Poor Jeff hadn't stood a chance.

And this time her wiles were clearly directed at his twin. Eyes narrowing, Guy leaned closer. If Blake was to be her next target, she'd miscalculated. Yet, as he opened his mouth to growl at her to back off, he caught a whiff of the sweet, intoxicating floral scent that was all she ever wore to bed. Hot blood rushed through his veins, pooling in his lower belly.

Ah, hell!

If only his body hated her, too…

With grim realism, Guy shut his mouth with a snap and decided it was just as well the resort was full to capacity. The crowds would make it easier for him to avoid her.

"Art sent me."

"Art sent you?"

The question must have betrayed his dazed disorientation

because Blake spoke from beside him, reminding Guy that he and Avery were not alone and that he'd asked Avery what she was doing here. "Avery is Art Lloyd's niece—even though she doesn't resemble him in the least."

Avery flashed a quick smile at Blake, and Guy could've sworn the woman fluttered her eyelashes at his brother. Damn her.

"You're Art's niece?" Disbelief was certainly better than following through on the overwhelming impulse to shove her away from his brother.

"Uh-huh." Avery nodded, and the wispy bangs shimmered with the lustre of gold in the sunshine. "I'm sure you're aware he was scheduled to speak at the gala, but he's ill. Flu on top of asthma and a weak chest. The doctor says he can't possibly fly in that condition."

He could've sworn he read apprehension in her wide, Barbie-blue eyes. Not that he blamed her. Even now, seven weeks after she'd run out on him, he wanted to shake her.

Instead he shoved his fists into his pockets and said, "I'm sorry to hear he's ill. I like Art."

He didn't need to add that he detested *her*. Avery wasn't stupid—if she didn't see it in his face, she'd be able to draw that inference herself.

She inhaled sharply.

Guy couldn't help himself, he looked down. The pink roses moved, her sweet floral scent surrounded him, and he could've sworn his world tilted, too.

From a distance he heard her say in that breathy, bedroom voice that drove him crazy, "Well, I'm here to speak in Art's place."

Hell!

Inside the snowy-white bower of the grand marquee the Friday night oyster-and-champagne cocktail party that launched the Food and Wine Gala each year was in full swing. Waitresses circulated with trays piled high with hors d'oevres, while dinner-jacketed waiters refilled tulip glasses that glinted in the light of the glittering crystal chandeliers overhead.

"Erica has outdone herself," Guy said with grudging approval to Blake as he scanned the chattering crowd who'd paid top dollar for tickets to tonight's event.

"It's the food that's got the crowd talking," said Blake, "and that's your domain."

Guy inclined his head in acceptance of the compliment. "It helps that every available ticket was sold," he pointed out. "The more people here tonight, the more media coverage the festival will get, and the more word-of-mouth buzz will spread."

"She's certainly better at public relations than we ever expected," his twin conceded. "But I was always certain there wouldn't be any tickets left over to give to the local business suppliers as Erica suggested."

"The gesture would've won Jarrod Ridge plenty of local goodwill." Guy had joined his twin in vetoing the suggestion when Erica had made it. Deep down Guy suspected he'd done it more because he resented his illegitimate half sister's very existence, rather than for sound business reasons. It was a suspicion that made him decidedly uncomfortable, one that he was not yet ready to confront.

"Anyway it would've made the function too big—lost the exclusivity." Blake sounded certain.

"We could've limited the number of speakers who gained complimentary entry." Guy's brooding gaze settled on the woman whose arrival earlier had turned his hard-won peace on its head. Avery didn't look like she had a care in the world. But he would've breathed a lot easier without her here tonight.

"Dad always gave festival speakers free entry to the opening night cocktail party. Mom set the tradition."

Blake's point hammered the final nail in the coffin. And Guy resisted the urge to argue that none of them had done what Don Jarrod wanted in life. So why the reverence for his opinion now that he was dead?

But the night of the official opening of the Food and Wine Gala was certainly not the time for friction with his twin.

Particularly not with Avery nearby. A sideways jerk of her head warned him she'd seen them. Guy edged closer to his brother. He fully intended to save his twin from Avery's irresistible advances tonight. And damn irresistible she was, too, in a dress the color of summer sunshine. Every time she moved diamond drop earrings sparkled through the pale gold feathers of her hair. Even in this celebrity-studded crowd she attracted attention.

After giving them a brief smile of greeting, Avery showed none of this morning's interest in Blake. From the corner of his eye Guy watched her intercept a tall, well-built stranger. His mouth twisted as she flung her arms around the man and kissed him on the cheek, before stepping away with a beaming smile.

It certainly hadn't taken her long to find company.

"Who's the man beside Avery Lancaster?" he demanded. His twin knew everyone worth knowing. Blake's networking skills and business acumen were unsurpassed.

"Looks familiar." Blake frowned with concentration. He snapped his fingers. "Got it. A vintner. From California—I think. But I can't recall his name."

"Which winery is he with? Does he grow good grapes?" It seemed important to establish a flaw in the stranger who stood too close to Avery for Guy's comfort.

Blake shook his head. "Can't remember. It will come to me. Why the interest?"

Guy refused to admit that he was fishing. Whoever Avery's quarry was, his highly polished Italian shoes and the avant-garde designer-label tuxedo he wore were a testimony to his wealth. It would be good to know that he had some weakness that could be exposed when needed. "Always good to know who's making the best wines."

"Information always gives us an edge over the competition," agreed Blake.

At that moment Avery threw her head back and laughed at something the Californian said. Her earrings danced and her eyes sparkled.

Unexpectedly, anger ignited in Guy's belly.

He swung away and told himself he should be relieved to be rid of a gold digger like Avery. So why the hell was he so damned annoyed? He'd always been easygoing about relationships, shrugging philosophically when they ended. And usually remaining friends with his former lovers.

But this time it was different.

Blake asked him something. He grunted his assent without any idea about what he'd agreed to. Then he told himself Avery had declared war by running out on him in New York without an explanation of why she'd seduced his business partner, his friend. He'd deserved to know. *She* might think it was over between them. But *he* wasn't through with her yet.

Not by a long shot.

No one betrayed him, then ran out on him…and Avery was about to learn that.

When Erica joined him and Blake, Guy shifted to get a clear view of Avery again as she accepted a glass of champagne that a waiter offered. She didn't take a sip.

A heartbeat later, Avery's head turned his way. Guy found himself blurting out to Erica that she'd done a great job with tonight's cocktail party before Avery could catch him staring at her with puppy-dog eyes. He didn't even notice his half sister's flush of surprised pleasure or Blake glaring daggers at him, reflecting the uneasy relationship between the Jarrod brothers and their new-found half-sister.

Another furtive glance showed that Avery had set her untouched glass of champagne down on the edge of the table behind her and was talking, gesturing with both her hands to illustrate what she was saying. When her fingertips settled on her companion's jacket sleeve, anger stabbed deep in Guy's chest. Forgetting to pretend disinterest, he assessed the easy familiarity of the gesture through narrowed, bitter eyes.

Maybe not a stranger after all.

A former lover? Someone she'd been pursuing even while she passed time in his own bed?

Bile rose in the back of Guy's throat.

"What's wrong?"

Guy started. Erica was gazing at him with concerned eyes.

He glanced around.

"Don't worry, Blake's not here. He's gone to fetch me a glass of water. I'm hot and thirsty. It's been a long day."

That made him feel curiously uncomfortable. He hadn't been aware of Erica's discomfort. Or his twin's departure. Because he'd been too damned busy devouring Avery with his eyes. Was he so transparent that even the half sister he barely knew could read him like a book? He pressed his lips together and glanced away without responding, discomforted by the sudden flush that heated his face.

"Who is she?"

"Nobody," Guy bit out.

Erica blinked. "Hey, I only wanted to help. You looked… unhappy."

Unhappy? Not at all. Instantly Guy forced a smile. "I'm fine."

She didn't look convinced.

"Truly, I am."

"Okay, I'll butt out." A smile softened the words.

His own smile widened into a relieved grin. "Thanks."

The lines of strain around her eyes eased, and a wave of remorse flooded him. It was time to cut Erica some slack. She'd done a damn fine job with the festival so far. Yet before he could offer an olive branch he caught sight of Avery and her companion heading for the exit. The tension that had been winding tighter ratcheted up another notch.

She wasn't ending up in the other man's bed tonight. Not under his nose, on his turf.

A well-known food writer stepped forward to greet Avery's companion, causing him to pause. Guy made his move.

"Excuse me," he murmured to Erica, before rapidly shouldering his way through the throng, unaware that his half sister watched him go, a bemused look on her face. His sole focus was on Avery.

"I want to speak to you." He cut Avery away from her partner as neatly as a wrangler.

"Guy! What are you doing?"

Placing his arm around her, he bent his head toward her. To an onlooker it would have appeared intimate. Even cozy. But his growled warning was anything but lover-like. "Now's not the time for a scene, Avery."

"Scene? I'm not making a scene—you are," she objected, her voice rising as he swept her along with him. *"Let go of me."*

He leaned closer still—and instantly her sweetly sexy floral scent surrounded him. Savagely fighting the sudden blast of raw desire, Guy lowered his voice and murmured into her ear, "Hush. I have no intention of kidnapping you."

Two

Avery wasn't so sure.

It only took one glance to reveal that there was a determined—even ruthless—set to Guy's jaw that she didn't recognize. His arm, heavy and unwelcome, tightened around her waist. She would've given anything not to be so spine-tinglingly aware of his proximity as he hurried her away from Matt.

She'd known this confrontation was coming from the moment he'd realized she was here to speak in Uncle Art's place. She'd tensed, waiting for the outburst that had never come.

If she'd realized that *her* Guy Jarrod was one of the Aspen Jarrods she'd have done whatever she could've to avoid coming here. Heck, even though it would've meant breaking her word to her uncle, she'd pleaded with Matt this afternoon to take his dad's spot so that she could catch the first flight out. But Matt had to be back in Napa Valley by tomorrow. And not even her desperate pleas had swayed him.

As she shot her nemesis a sideways glance, her breath snagged in her throat. From the opposite end of the grand marquee he'd been eye-catching, but up close Guy Jarrod was utterly devastating. His six-foot plus height suited the tailored tuxedo, the broad shoulders tapering to a lean waist, while the white dress shirt only emphasized the masculine perfection of his handsome profile.

I should hate him…he deserves it.

To hide the humiliating effect his body had on her, she wrinkled her brow, hoping she looked convincingly puzzled. "What did you want to talk about?"

Guy clearly wasn't fooled. His lips firmed into an impatient line as he stopped in the back corner of the marquee beside a table laden with trays of oysters. He turned to face her. "You taking Art's place."

"Is it a problem?"

Of course it was. His reaction earlier had shown that. What she couldn't work out was why he didn't want her speaking at the Food and Wine Gala. Well, she was no doubt about to learn.

Avery forced herself to smile faintly—and very politely—at him before helping herself to a glass from a passing waiter to give her hands something to do. She took a delicate sip of the pale liquid and pretended to savor the crisp dryness on her tongue.

Guy's gaze dipped to her mouth. The eyes that met hers a moment later had gone dark. In the past he'd sometimes poured a glass of champagne for them to share after—

No! She wasn't thinking of the countless abandoned glasses of untouched champagne or the passionate encounters that had followed.

Her lashes fell, and Avery fixed her attention on the square

black snaps of his dress shirt. She recognized those snaps…
one evening she'd yanked them all loose—

Oh, heavens!

She jerked her head back and focused on his jaw instead.
It was a hard jaw, a determined j—

"You're not listening."

"Of course I'm listening." Please don't let him ask her to
repeat whatever he'd just said.

"You're not even interested."

"Not in you," she muttered rebelliously.

Only a few inches separated his mouth from the area of
jaw line she'd been examining, and she watched his beautiful
lips flatten into a hard line. To her exasperation, her heartbeat
kicked up. This close he smelled so familiar. Of sandalwood
soap, a green hint of moss…and man. But this recklessly
rash awareness of the man didn't alter the fact that he was a
first-class bastard.

One she would be wise to avoid at all costs.

"How typical of a woman not to be able to separate her
emotions from her work."

What? "That's not true—" Avery broke off. Or maybe it
was. She'd made it personal by disavowing any interest in
him. "Okay, I shouldn't have made that crack." Especially
when her reaction suggested it was patently, horrifyingly
untrue.

She was pathetic.

Hadn't she learned what kind of scum Guy Jarrod was,
despite the fancy French restaurant he owned in New York
and his high-society family?

God help her….

He rocked back on his heels and the extra inches of space
allowed her respite to breathe again without drowning in
his scent. For an awful moment she thought he was going to
pursue exactly how much of a lie her denial had been.

To her relief, he let it slide.

"No, you shouldn't have. And I'll accept that as an apology."

She wouldn't have gone so far as to call it an apology. Annoyance made her bristle like a cat stroked the wrong way. "That's big of you."

He expelled an impatient sigh. "You know, this isn't going to work. Go back to California—I'll find someone else to stand in for Art."

Avery stared at him, aghast. This was what she'd wanted… but now that he was telling her to go, she knew there was no way she could ever tell Art she'd let him down. "I promised Art—"

Guy was shaking his head. "Art and I were scheduled to do two talks together," he said, "and it's clear that you're not going to be able to cooperate."

Oh, dear God, what had Art gotten her into? He'd muttered something about a panel on wine selection and a presentation about the importance of superior service in a world-class establishment but that had been all. There'd been no mention of a joint presentation with anyone, let alone Guy Jarrod.

She should never have come….

Uncle Art's pleading voice played through her head. She hadn't had a choice. To think she'd considered speaking at such a prestigious event, the opportunity of a lifetime. But this wasn't about her…it was about what she owed Uncle Art and Aunt Tilly.

She'd never lived up to Aunt Tilly's hopes. But Uncle Art was proud of her. He'd taken her in after his sister and brother-in-law—had died in a sailing accident. He'd loved her, cherished her, supported her. For her uncle she would walk across burning embers—barefoot. Except he'd never asked that of her.

He'd run interference on her behalf with Aunt Tilly when

she'd refused to attend another beauty pageant or talent show. He'd supported her when she'd bailed out of drama school. He'd never asked anything of her.

Until now.

Her shoulders sagged. "Of course I'll cooperate with you." Within reason. *No sex with his friends and colleagues.* More to the point, no sex with Guy Jarrod. Period. "Just tell me what you need me to do."

"Have an oyster."

They'd decadently shared oysters in bed one memorable Monday when Baratin had been closed. They'd risen late. He'd fed them to her...interspersed with kisses...it had ended up in one of the most erotic encounters of her life. Surely he wasn't referring to that?

It took a moment for the shocked daze to clear and for Avery to realize he was holding out a platter where oysters on the half shell nestled between fat wedges of lemon and translucent ice cubes.

"They're perfectly shucked. I oversaw the preparation myself. No sand or broken shells. Just succulent flesh with a hint of juice."

For a brief second she caught a glimpse of the Guy she'd thought she'd known so well. Wicked mirth sparkled in his gray-black eyes and warmed her.

Irresistible, damn him.

She resisted the charm with a toss of her head. "No, thanks. I'm quite sated."

The laughter evaporated. "I'm sure you are."

The platter disappeared into the hands of a hovering waiter. Avery searched Guy's face but could find no trace of the bitterness the words suggested. She must've imagined it.

"My schedule for the next couple of weeks of the festival is ferocious." Guy continued as if they'd never shared that crazy moment. "Art offered to do most of the work to put the first presentation together."

That got her back on track. That's why he didn't want her speaking? He considered her too inept, did he? Believed she couldn't do what Art had undertaken to do? Avery suspected she was going to regret not leaping at the opportunity of escape Guy offered. Instead, her innate love for a challenge surged, and she found herself saying, "I can do that."

He didn't look convinced. In fact, he looked downright dubious. "Not only was Art doing two talks with me, he had a solo presentation planned."

"On the importance of superior service—I know."

"And he was contracted to look over the resort's wine lists and compile a report of his findings about service levels," Guy continued as though she hadn't interrupted. "It will have to wait until he's fit to come out here himself."

"No, it won't. Art and I discussed this, I'll do it in his place. That won't be any problem at all."

A waiter offered Guy a glass of champagne. Unconsciously Avery noted that the waiter's white jacket was pristine and carefully pressed, his handling of the tray deft. The resort staff were evidently well-trained.

Guy glanced at her still-full glass before helping himself from the proffered tray. "It's a pity I don't share your confidence," he said in a clipped voice, and Avery's approving smile to the waiter froze.

She turned her full attention back to the man whose reappearance in her life had caused such inner turmoil, caused so many memories and emotions, which she'd thought she'd suppressed, to waken.

"Oh?"

Avery cringed and dropped her gaze to stare at the bubbles rising merrily in the pale golden liquid in her own glass. *Oh?* Was that the best she could do? What had happened to her intelligence? Her wit? Her sass? Was she going to let this arrogant jerk walk all over her?

She was the one with a problem, not him!

She *hated* him.

Blindly she set her glass down.

She would be professional. Reasonable. And blow him away with her expertise. "Look, I've overhauled plenty of wine lists, I've trained junior sommeliers and other staff, I've done lots of public speaking." She jabbed her right index finger against the fingers of her left hand as she counted off the list. "I've taught, and I've even had my own TV show. That should boost your confidence a little."

"The TV show lasted all of four episodes."

Avery colored. The show had been axed. Because the ratings hadn't been good enough, she'd been told. She suspected there could have been more episodes—if she'd been prepared to sleep with the producer, when he'd made that suggestion. But that price had been too high. Avery had quit—despite Aunt Tilly's disappointment. And the producer had found another—more accommodating—sommelier. It hadn't surprised Avery when that show had ended in scandal and tears. Losing the program hadn't been the first time her sex-kitten looks had mucked up her life.

Even Guy was giving her the kind of once-over that left her enraged…and uncharacteristically flustered. But by the time his gaze came back to meet her own furious gaze, his was filled with contempt. And something else. Something that caused her heart to leap.

Avery resisted it.

There was no room for this…this…unwanted feeling. She was over Guy Jarrod. He was a bastard. And she had no intention of ever returning to the misery he'd caused her.

She could do this. She knew it. But first she had to convince him.

Lifting her chin a notch, she readied herself for a fight. "*Cuisine* stated that the new wine list at your New York restaurant had been put together 'with artistry and sophisticated style'. I wouldn't deliver anything less here."

"This isn't Baratin, Avery. Jarrod Ridge has four restaurants and six bars. The selection of wines, beers and alcoholic beverages served in each of those needs to be overhauled, as you put it. Don't forget I've read your résumé. You've never handled a project of this scope."

He didn't blink as he delivered his verdict in a calm, controlled voice. Avery knew he didn't believe she was up for the task. She forced herself not to look away from that alarming scrutiny. "I'm sure I can discuss whether I'm capable of completing the task with whoever is in charge of overseeing the menus and service requirements."

"That would be me." His crooked smile held no amusement, even if it did cause two nearby women to give him admiring glances. "I'm looking at introducing new dishes, and the beverages need to be matched to give a perfect selection."

"I'd be working with *you?*"

He nodded and raised his glass. "Do you want to toast to the success of our partnership?" The irony was acute.

Two could play that game. Avery reached for the glass on the table behind her and raised it with bravado.

"To success!"

Champagne splashed out, almost landing on her yellow silk dress.

"Careful!" Guy gripped her wrist with his free hand and the crisis was averted.

"Thanks," she murmured. "I would've hated to have ruined this dress."

"That didn't augur well." He quirked an eyebrow. "Still want to stay?"

In truth, she was ready to run. She'd never admit that. Especially not to him.

"Of course." She tilted up her chin. "You won't get rid of me that easily."

A fierce and stormy emotion flickered across his face. Then his thumb moved against her wrist, and his hold eased a degree. The frisson of awareness that shot through her was as unwelcome as the knowledge that they'd be working together—far too closely for Avery's comfort—for the duration of her stay.

It would be an impossible situation.

She raised her hand, his fell away, and she took a gulp of champagne. Then sneezed.

"Steady."

Her eyes were streaming.

"The bubbles always make me sneeze."

"How unfortunate for a sommelier!"

She wiped her tears away with her fingertips. "That's what my family thinks, too. It's one downside of the job."

"That's why you've barely drunk any tonight—and why you never wanted champagne in the past."

Arrested by his statement, Avery stared at him. He'd been watching her. For how long? And…why?

How could she work with a man she'd once upon a time hoped she was falling in love with? A man to whom her body unfurled like a sunflower to the sun. A man she now hated.

"Here, let me take that."

Numbly she opened her hand and relinquished the glass. Guy set it back down on the table behind them.

How could she let Uncle Art down? He'd been the rock in her life. How could she turn her back on him when *he* needed *her?*

Avery swallowed. The short answer was, she couldn't.

"So—" Guy faced her again "—you're staying then."

She swallowed her objections. "I can take the heat in the kitchen," she said rashly, "can you?"

There was a moment of throbbing silence. Then he said softly, "I can take anything you care to dish out."

"You're the chef, you're the expert at dishing out."

Avery didn't care if he heard her disillusionment. Between Guy and his friend Jeff they'd shattered the dreams she'd spun around the man in front of her, the man she'd convinced herself was her perfect life partner.

That night Guy had sent Jeff to her for her birthday had made her grow up....

Pushing past him, she said, "Now, I need to go find Matt."

Three

Day one down…just over three weeks more to endure.

Yet despite her dread about Guy's presence, Avery had managed to successfully avoid him and her first full day at the Jarrod Ridge Food and Wine Gala had passed in a buzz of excitement. She'd found herself indulging in celebrity spotting like some wide-eyed teenager. There'd been the handsome hero of a popular soap, a pop diva with rainbow-streaked hair and a hunky, tanned tennis star.

In the afternoon, she'd sidled in to listen to the presentation her cousin Matt was giving, and joined him in the trendy sky lounge on the covered rooftop of Jarrod Manor for a too-quick drink afterward.

"This is the kind of world Mom always wanted for you, pumpkin." Matt stretched his legs and lounged back in the leather armchair. "She was certain you'd be a star."

Avery wrinkled her nose. "Despite all the classes, I never had any acting talent. I would've made an awful beauty queen—too short. And you know I hate being called pumpkin. I'm twenty-seven years old." But there was no heat in the objection that had already been made a million times before.

Matt chuckled—as she'd known he would. "You really did look like a pumpkin when you arrived to live with us. Chubby and wearing orange dungarees—don't know why Mom ever thought you'd win any of those baby pageants."

"Chubby? Oh, you!" But she laughed up into his teasing face. "I was two—hardly a baby. And it's your fault Aunt Tilly craved a little girl, you were all such hooligans." As much as the four scruffy boys had overwhelmed her in the beginning, she'd grown to love them all—even her well-meaning aunt. El Dorado, the boutique vineyard her uncle had acquired shortly before her arrival, had become home.

"When do you leave for home?" Her cousins still based themselves at El Dorado—as did she when in California.

"I fly out first thing in the morning." Matt unfolded himself from the armchair and rose, yawning, to his full height. "I've still got to prepare for my meeting tomorrow."

Avery scrambled to her feet.

"I wish you could stay longer." A wistful note crept into her voice. It was cowardly wishing Matt would stay to help her cope with Guy. Yet his departure felt like a desertion.

"No chance, pumpkin." Matt threw an affectionate arm around her shoulders. "It was hard enough taking these two days out my schedule, but it was worth the exposure that today's talk gave the business."

"You did great."

She gave Matt a fierce hug and hoped he hadn't detected the desperation behind it. Those hopes were dashed as he held her at arm's length and studied her face.

"Dad will be okay." All teasing vanished, leaving his

expression unexpectedly serious. "Don't wear yourself down with worry."

He'd sensed her unease but he'd attributed it to the wrong cause. Immediately guilt constricted her chest. She'd been so busy fretting about Guy, she'd hardly spared a thought for her uncle. Selfish!

Taking a deep breath she said. "Make sure your dad looks after himself. I don't like that he's ill."

"He's a tough old codger." Matt gave her a squeeze. "He'll be fine—you'll see. Mom will coddle him to death. But I'll give him your love when I see him tomorrow."

Over Matt's arm Avery found herself looking into a pair of stormy eyes. Guy Jarrod. Then the shutters came down, and all expression leached out, leaving her wondering if she'd imagined the flash of emotion.

Ignore him, she commanded herself. He's not worth the heartache. She hoped she'd be able to follow her own advice in the weeks to come.

Avery made herself glance away from Guy's blank stare to give her cousin a wobbly smile. "I've decided to spoil myself. I've booked a massage at the resort spa and I'll have a soak in a hot tub afterwards. That should guarantee I'll sleep like a baby tonight."

"I suspect you haven't done enough of that lately."

"What do you mean?" She stared at her cousin in surprise.

"I'm not going to pry, but you came back from New York looking like a wraith. It was all we could do to stop Mom interrogating you."

Avery felt herself flush. "You're joking!"

"We love you, pumpkin. You're family. If I ever meet the man who put that bruised look in your eyes, I'll be giving him a few bruises of his own."

Matt's tone was light but his eyes were deadly serious. She

didn't dare glance past him to see where Guy was. If Matt knew that Guy had expected her to sleep with his friend, before returning to join the ménage à trois himself, her cousin would be ready to kill him.

She gave a dismissive laugh. "He was nothing!"

"Get over him," Matt said gruffly.

"Oh, I intend to." She smiled at him. "When you see me again I'll be heart-whole and fancy-free. Who knows, later in the week I might go shopping...do a little sightseeing."

"Or find yourself a hot lover."

"Matthew!"

"If you're going to live it up, pumpkin," Matt grinned down at her, "Aspen is the place to do it. Indulge yourself. No regrets. And, don't worry, I'll keep you updated about Dad."

"Thanks, you're the best." She stood on tiptoes and brushed her lips across his cheek in a gesture of gratitude and affection.

Giving up on wrestling her foolish need to search out Guy, Avery turned her head. To her relief the man who had haunted her nightmares was nowhere to be seen.

The sight of brass letters on the wall announcing Tranquility Spa was enough to ease some of the diabolical tension that had been building ever since Avery's encounter with Guy yesterday.

The first thing Avery noticed was the calming sound of water as she entered the spa. Water trickled down stone fountains set in wall panels along the reception area. Between the fountains scenic paintings formed vistas of incredible beauty.

Two women were talking behind a long counter carved from pale, polished wood, and one turned as the front door clicked shut.

"Avery?"

The gold badge the woman wore read Melissa Jarrod, Manager. With her long, wavy blond hair and blue eyes there was little resemblance to Guy's dark hair and metallic, almost black, eyes. Perhaps Melissa Jarrod was a cousin or married to one of his brothers.

Giving a hesitant smile, Avery said, "Yes, I have an appointment for a massage."

Melissa glanced at the flat computer screen on the desk, and said to the nervous-looking woman beside her, "Rita, would you let Joanie know her client is here? I'm going to leave now, I'm so tired I can barely stand." With a sweet smile to Avery she said, "Let me show you where your treatment room is."

Melissa did look pale, Avery thought as she followed the other woman down a corridor where smaller wall fountains were set between wooden doors.

"You're in the Red Room," said Melissa. "The saunas and steam rooms are further along. I'd recommend fifteen minutes in one of the steam rooms after your massage, followed by a soak in a hot tub."

"Sounds fabulous." Avery had every intention of following that advice.

Melissa pushed the next door along open, and Avery glimpsed an interior painted a shade of welcoming red ochre. A huge seascape of a dramatic sunset dominated one wall, while a dark red massage bed with a soft throw stood in the foreground. Farther back sprawled a large, wood-paneled hot tub with an ice bucket resting in a black wrought-iron stand beside it. Three fat white candles cast a soft glow, adding to the womb-like warmth of the room.

"Oh, wow!"

The other woman laughed. "You may have gathered that our mission at Tranquility Spa is to ensure that you relax."

Avery stepped into the embrace of the warm, sensuous room and gave a sigh of contentment.

"Can I pour you a glass of champagne?"

"No, but I'll definitely help myself to some of those while I soak." Avery pointed to the tray of dark chocolate truffles at the side of the tub. "What a heavenly, decadent treat."

"You can change out of your clothes." Melissa was smiling as she handed Avery a soft towel. "Joanie will be here in a few minutes to give you your massage."

The massage passed in a delightful haze of well-being. Avery felt her muscles easing as the pent-up tightness dissipated under Joanie's skilled fingers. Guy had loved stroking his hands along her back when they made love....

Yes, if she was brutally truthful, she'd missed the passion they'd shared. Missed laughing with him at the end of a day when they sat in the massive tub in his starkly modern apartment after sating themselves in his king-size bed. But she hadn't been prepared to pay the cost that Guy had demanded.

A cost she'd never expected.

His promise that he had a surprise in store for her birthday had caused a surge of hope...after all, she'd fallen for him like a ton of bricks. Even though she'd sensed his reticence about commitment, she'd hoped...

He'd promised a surprise.

It was her birthday.

Maybe...

Avery had been almost too scared to hope.

Yet when she'd opened the door of Guy's apartment that evening, the last thing she'd expected had been Jeff. She'd met Guy's business partner twice before. Briefly. He'd seemed pleasant enough. What she had managed to piece together was that Guy and Jeff had started Go Green fueled by a desire to create a place where consumers could find all-green cookware and cooking technology for a green, clean diet. Avery loved the concept…and Guy was convinced that the corporation was already making a difference to people's mindsets.

Yet the Jeff bouncing up and down on the doorstep hardly resembled the mild man she'd encountered previously.

"Yes?" she asked.

"Guy asked me to drop in, he's been held up at Baratin."

Typical. Guy had gotten into the workaholic groove at his beloved Baratin and spending time with her on her birthday had been shoved onto the back burner.

Quashing her qualms about letting Jeff in, Avery stepped back. "Come in."

Jeff followed her through the sky-lit lobby where the white walls were lined with modern abstracts into a spacious lounge with polished dark-wood floors, leather furniture and floor-to-ceiling windows.

"I'm to escort you down to Baratin for your birthday dinner in—" Jeff glanced at his ornate watch "—just under an hour."

So Guy hadn't forgotten about her birthday. The leap of joy was quickly followed by a feeling of letdown. He hadn't cared enough to collect her himself for their date.

"Thank you, that's very kind of you."

Jeff flung himself down onto the closest couch and grinned up at her. "I try."

"Can I get you a drink?"

"Bourbon. Neat. On ice. Thanks."

Avery crossed to the tallboy that housed Guy's bar. The clink of ice cubes followed by the gurgle of bourbon filling the glass broke the silence. When she turned it was to find Jeff examining her in a way he'd never done before.

A frisson of discomfort feathered along her spine.

Stop it. He's Guy's friend, his business partner, someone he trusts, she told herself. She handed the drink to Jeff. Before she could retreat his free hand snaked out and he hauled her onto his lap.

Then he was kissing her, wet, alcohol-drenched kisses that made her stomach turn, muttering fantasies that made her cringe. A furious struggle, and she was on her feet.

"Get out."

He stood. "Don't be so hasty, sweetheart."

Avery was trembling with outrage, fear…and something else.

"Go, and don't come back." She backed away. A glance showed her that her cell phone lay on the sideboard. "I'm calling Guy."

Jeff laughed. "That's not going to help you."

"What do you mean?"

"He knows, sweetheart."

Avery froze, her heart thumping in her chest. "Knows what?"

"He sent me, remember?"

"To play taxi driver." She tossed her hair back.

"Oh, you are an innocent." It didn't sound such a good thing the way Jeff said it—and the way his eyes roved over her made her feel grubby. "Despite that fantastically sexy little body."

"Guy wouldn't want to hear you saying things like that."

He laughed again. "Guy sent me. I'm your birthday present."

Horror shook her. "What do you mean?"

"Guy sent me to pleasure you. I'm to chauffeur you to Baratin when we're done. Then we were going to feed you your favourite foods." He licked his lips suggestively. "Afterwards all three of us were going to share dessert." There was no mistaking his meaning. "Guy wanted it to be a birthday you'd never forget."

Jeff reached for her.

"No!" She slapped his hand away.

His face contorted. "Come here."

As his hands clamped down on her shoulders, Avery kicked him in the shins.

"Ouch, you—"

She didn't wait to hear more. The front door seemed a mile away but she made it. Once outside she looked both ways before bolting for the stairwell. And cocked her head to listen, while her heartbeat slowed, until she was sure that Jeff hadn't followed.

Then she brushed her fingers across her eyes, surprised to find no residue of tears.

This had been Guy's surprise?

Even now, lying facedown on the massage bed, surrounded by the soft light of scented candles, she could still remember the maelstrom of emotions that had shaken her that night. By gifting his friend to her for the evening of her birthday and expecting her to sleep with Jeff, Guy had destroyed her trust.

Yet meeting him again here at Jarrod Ridge had proved she wasn't immune from his effect on her, that she still desired him.

That discovery horrified her.

What kind of woman did that make her? How could she lust after such a jerk? And how could she reconcile that with her most secret desire for a loving husband and a clutch of tow-haired kids?

"Here's a terry robe."

Joanie's voice stirred Avery from the conundrum threatening to short-circuit her brain. "Thank you."

Turning away, the masseuse said, "I'll fill the tub with hot water. The steam rooms are down the hall from the massage rooms. You can leave your belongings in here. I'll give you an access card to get back in."

The next fifteen minutes passed in a haze of heat. Avery couldn't help thinking of the conversation she'd had with Matt.

"Get over him," Matt had said.

And Avery was determined to do just that. By the time she left Jarrod Ridge it would be without a backward glance. She would exorcise this wretched awareness of the man. She would banish him from her thoughts…no matter what it took.

By the time Avery exited the steam room, filled with resolve, a sheen of moisture dewed her skin.

As she reached into the pocket of the robe for the access card to the treatment room where she'd had her massage, a masculine hand came down on the door in front of her, blocking her entry. Avery found herself face to face with the man who'd occupied so much of her recent thoughts.

"I've been looking for you. Rita said you were here." Guy's face was harder, more remote, than she'd ever seen it. The only evidence of the humor and amiability that had been so dear to her back in New York lay in the laugh creases around his eyes.

For a fragment of time her heart ached for what had been, what might have been, what was now forever lost.

No sign of laughter lingered in the steely gaze that roamed her giving no quarter. Avery became conscious that her face was cleansed of makeup and the spa's white robe ended inches above her knees.

"I see you've already managed to find yourself a rich lover."

Avery froze. Then, not deigning to answer, she knocked his hand off the door and pushed past him, seeking the sanctuary of the private room.

But Guy was quicker. Before she could slam the door in his face and lock it, he was inside, and his foot kicked the door shut behind him.

Balmy steam from the hot tub cocooned them, adding another dimension to the tension that pulsed between them. The warm reds that had appeared so welcoming suddenly seemed sensual and sultry. Avery's heart started to pound. An acute feeling of vulnerability swamped her. She drew the toweling robe more tightly around her.

"Get out, Guy."

Guy stalked closer. "Yesterday I thought it was my brother you were after. But by last night you'd found someone else. Did he share your bed?"

"What?"

"The Californian."

"Californian—" Realization dawned. He was talking about Matt.

"Did he touch you? Love you?" The darkening eyes smoldered in the glow of the candlelight. "Pleasure you?" His hand came up and stroked her skin, causing a rush of shivers to follow in its wake.

Guy thought Matt was her lover.

Avery almost laughed. Then she took in the tight-pressed mouth, the flexing muscle in his jaw.

Help…he believed it. And it had made him furious.

His fury ignited her own.

What right did he have to judge her? To leap to conclusions? She launched into attack. "Why?" she asked softly. "Are you jealous?"

The dark tumult in his eyes turned to flame.

In that instant a truly outrageous realization stunned her. Guy *was* jealous! Not because he cared for her, but because he thought she was sharing her body with someone else. Someone he hadn't sanctioned…

Bastard!

"You—" His grim voice broke off as he advanced on her.

A thrill of all-too familiar and totally unwanted electricity shot through Avery. She stood her ground, refusing to back away. He was close, so close that she could feel the force of his breath, smell the tangy male scent of him, all intensified by the steam rising from the freshly filled hot tub.

His hands gripped her shoulders. Before she could protest, his mouth slanted across hers.

Mindful of her resolve to free herself of his thrall, Avery kept her lips primly shut, yet Guy made no attempt to force entry. Instead, after the first press, his lips softened, teasing hers, pressing little kisses along the sensitive seam. Despite her determination to resist him, he was too seductive. Every bit as good as she remembered from the halcyon days before it had all turned to dust. The familiar warmth lazily uncurled in her stomach and spread through her, leaving her craving more.

Too soon he'd raised his head.

"Did *he* kiss you like that last night?"

Before she could tell him that Matt wasn't her lover but her cousin—almost a brother—that she'd grown up with, Guy's mouth was back on hers. Hot. Voracious. Devouring. Her hands crept up around his neck, caressing the smooth male skin with her fingertips. He pulled back and sucked in a shuddering breath.

"No one kisses like that," she whispered into the cavern of space that separated them.

The vibrating tension in his body eased a fraction. A hand cupped her cheek and he tilted her head back. Avery closed her eyes…waiting…waiting for his mouth to descend again.

"Look at me!"

Her lashes fluttered up. Reluctantly she met his gaze. An indefinable emotion lurked in the turbulent depths. Despite the warmth of the spa room, and the steam swirling around them, Avery shivered. This was not the easy-going restaurateur she'd thought herself in love with. She didn't know this man.

"Not even Jeff?" he asked.

"What?" Avery blinked up at him in confusion.

"Forgotten how he kisses already?" There was a caustic bite to his tone.

"N-no."

Forgotten? *Guy sent me. I'm your birthday present.* Then Jeff had breathed over her with boozy breath and touched her with hands that made her feel unclean. The words that had spewed from his mouth had made her feel dirty to her soul. *I'm to chauffeur you to Baratin when we're done.*

How could she ever forget?

Was Guy jealous of the man he'd all but pimped her to? Well, she hoped he'd suffered the tortures of the damned. He'd destroyed her illusions. If he was jealous now, it was his own damn fault for opening a forbidden box that should have stayed shut.

He deserved to suffer.

The temptation to inflame his sexual possessiveness was too much. Avery gave him what she hoped looked like a seductive, kittenish smile. "I never kiss and tell."

"You did more than kiss Jeff. You slept with him."

She stretched her eyes wide. "Why the curiosity? Wish you'd been there? We almost called you to join in."

The instant the words left her lips, Avery experienced a rush of regret. She'd thrown away the opportunity to tell Guy the real truth about how much she'd hated what had happened that fateful night.

But how could she recant now? How could she tell him her

sarcasm had been prompted by hurt and anger at his ready acceptance that she'd slept with a man he'd sent to her? Pride wouldn't let her.

Hc could go to hcll.

Guy didn't love her. Had never loved her. It was enough to make her want to weep.

"Jeff told me that you'd been chasing him for weeks, and that night he couldn't resist what you were offering."

What?

Had he not sent Jeff to her? She gazed at Guy, searching for a chink in his shuttered face. But the only softness came from the flickering candlelight that danced over his skin, causing shadows to lurk under his cheekbones.

"That I offered?" she prompted.

Guy pushed a hand through his hair. "I was busy—"

"You were always busy."

His jaw tensed. "Jeff called just as I was about to ring you to ask you to catch a cab. He offered to make the call for me and get the cab so I could finish what I was doing. I thought it was important." His mouth twisted in a parody of a smile.

"So Jeff called me," she said flatly.

"And you asked him to pick you up—only when he got there did he find out what you had in mind."

"Of course." Avery felt numb. He'd believed Jeff.

The man must be dumb. How could he not know what they'd discovered was special? Something she'd never found with another man? Yet he believed her capable of sleeping with Jeffrey…and Matt…at the drop of a hat.

She shivered.

"You're cold."

Not cold. Goosebumps from reaction. She was hurting, exposed and vulnerable. Unlike him.

"Get into the hot tub," he ordered.

"With you here?"

He raised a dark eyebrow. "Why not? There's nothing I haven't seen many times before."

The biting sarcasm made her see red. All the objections that threatened to spill over fizzled out when he hit a button on the control dial and the jets started to froth.

Why not?

She'd told Matt that she was going to exorcise him.

No time better than the present.

With a reckless awareness of playing with fire, Avery dropped her terry robe. She was naked beneath. She heard Guy suck in air, but refused to turn her head to gauge his response. Instead she stepped over the lip of the tub into the churning water of the sunken spa.

And wondered if she'd ventured too far…

Guy could've sworn his heart ceased when Avery's robe slipped down her glorious body.

Any hope he'd nursed that Avery had not been playing cruel games with him and Jeff as her pawns had been extinguished by the brazen admission that she'd seduced poor Jeff.

It only took a glimpse of her naked form for the rage to flare into mind-blowing sexual hunger. Given that she was so little, Avery had the longest damned legs he'd ever seen. His eyes followed the sleek bare length to the delectable curve of her butt. She was perfect. Absolutely god-dammed perfect.

He wanted her. Damn, he ached with wanting. It had been too long….

The tub swallowed her as she settled down, the long legs and curvy body disappearing beneath the frothing water that gleamed in the light of the candles. She leaned her head against the edge of the tub and gave a sigh.

Only the top of her breasts were visible, yet even that was enough to make him hard.

After her betrayal he'd told her he never wanted to see her again. He'd been certain if he saw her, he'd throttle her. Famous last words. No doubt she planned to make him eat them, morsel by morsel. Well, here he was achingly aroused and dying to kiss that sassy provocative mouth again.

Damn.

She was here for the duration of the Food and Wine Gala. Why not sate this inconvenient hunger for her that gnawed at his gut like a wild, feral beast? This time he would make her as mad for him as she'd made poor, broken Jeff. The fool had risked everything for her. His friendship with Guy. Their business, Go Green.

Guy had been ready to plant a fist in Jeff's face for his perfidy until he'd realized how bad his friend had it. Jeff had told him about how Avery had teased and tempted him for weeks, until he'd been unable to resist her summons.

What would he have done if Avery had opened the door in nothing more than the bustier and G-string Jeff had told him she'd worn to welcome him?

Guy could understand Jeff's desperation. Would he have reacted any differently to her seduction? Hell, if he climbed into that spa beside her, he'd touch her and it would be over in moments.

Dragging in a breath he wrestled for control. Instead of allowing himself to be drawn into her trap, he dropped to his knees beside the sunken tub and started to knead her shoulders. This time it would be on his terms.

Avery started, she moaned.

"Good?"

"Mmm."

"Relax, let the warm water ease all the cricks."

"I already had a massage—that helped," she murmured so softly he had to bend forward to catch the words. "But how can I resist?"

Guy could see the edge of her pouting mouth. Her hair fell in soft tendrils about her face, and her features had relaxed.

He growled, a rough, throaty sound. "I better tell my sister to start a service offering neck rubs in the tub."

"Melissa is your sister? You mentioned brothers yesterday. I didn't even know you had a sister."

"You never asked," he pointed out.

"I suppose."

"We had better things to talk about."

It was true, he realized as he massaged her flesh. Their focus had been on the white-hot passion that had exploded between them, consuming them in an affair that had erupted before they could draw breath—let alone get to know each other.

But her silence made him feel a pang of guilt. Maybe they should've talked more…

"I've got another sister, too," he offered. "Erica. She's my half sister actually." He still wasn't sure how he felt about Erica. Until now he'd maintained a friendly, but definitely cool, distance. "We only discovered her existence after my father died."

"I heard about your father. I'm sorry."

His father had died less than a week after she'd slept with Jeff and walked out on him. It had been the worst week of his life. But Avery didn't need to know that.

"We weren't close." Guy dismissed her sympathy.

"It must've still been hard to discover he had another child."

"It was." Guy forced himself not to be abrupt. "The knowledge that my father had an affair so soon after mom's death was—" He broke off, reluctant to supply the words that might reveal any lingering vulnerability.

After a moment's pause, Avery said carefully, "It must have been hard for Erica, too."

Her voice held no judgment, she simply stated a fact. He wished he could see her expression. "It couldn't have been too bad for her. She inherited an equal share in Dad's estate. She's a wealthy woman now."

"Money isn't everything."

Avery of all people expected him to swallow that?

Guy found a knot and rubbed it, and Avery winced. He slowed his movements, his fingers lingering on flesh that had taken a golden glow under the candlelight.

"Erica found love, too." A note of cynicism entered his voice. "She's engaged to Christian Hanford now. The family lawyer," he tacked on, in case he wasn't making sense. Stroking her skin had that effect on him. Touching her made him forget everything else existed.

She was undoubtedly a sorceress. A magic woman who held him trapped in her secret sensuality.

"Where are you staying?" Guy changed the subject. He didn't want to talk about Erica, about the uncomfortable emotions his father's affair aroused and the sense of helpless loss that his father's death evoked.

"At Jarrod Manor," she replied, a little drowsily.

"So am I."

Avery stiffened under the stroke of his fingers. "Oh."

"Relax," he said. "It's the largest lodge. No danger of finding me—unless you want to." He didn't add that he was staying in one of the family suites on the top floor, which had their own card-access elevator. There was little chance of Avery's finding his suite by accident.

"But you only need to ask reception to find out where I'm staying—you're a Jarrod, they'd tell you whatever you wanted."

His hands stilled. "Do you want me to ask?"

"No!"

The water swirled around her as she moved in agitation. For a brief instant Guy caught a glimpse of pale pink nipple before she hastily sank beneath the bubbling water.

"On second thought, you probably don't even need to ask, do you? You'd have access to all the computer and reservation systems—and key cards."

"I'd never enter your room—or any guest's room—without an invitation." Guy was appalled by her assumption that he'd abuse his position—or the privacy of a guest. "You'd have to ask."

"Promise?"

The look she slanted up at him almost undid him. "Yes!"

She relaxed with a sigh, her head dropping back against the lip of the bath, the candlelight giving her blonde hair a rich patina. "I believe you."

I believe you. Her instant trust caused a rush of elation. Wordlessly, he rubbed his fingers in little circles along the apex of her shoulders, seeking out the tell-tale knots, massaging them. Her flesh was soft and supple beneath his fingers, and he savored the subtle, flowery scent that clung behind her ears, released by the sultry, heat of the steam, tempting him to set his lips against the silken skin.

Guy let out the breath he'd been holding. The tendrils at her nape lifted, and a rush of gooseflesh danced across her skin.

Unable to resist, he bent his head and placed his mouth against her nape.

Avery gave an audible gasp.

But no objection followed. He parted his lips and planted a row of open-mouthed kisses on her water-dewed skin, aware of the sound of her quickening breathing. His hands slipped forward around the curve of her body, and his fingers trailed over the soft, rounded mounds of her breasts.

She drew a sharp, jagged breath.

"Avery," he whispered, "invite me to join you in that damned tub."

Four

The one thing that Avery had learned about Guy in the month she'd shared his apartment in New York was that every inch of his body was pure, sinful temptation…and she was incapable of resisting any of it.

Tonight was no exception.

But tonight she knew exactly what she was doing…knew that this was not about dreams—only desire…and getting over Guy. She'd think of it as therapy.

"Join me?" she invited, her pulse skittering. "There's plenty of space."

"I thought you'd never ask."

He was already on his feet. The jeans and T-shirt he wore were discarded in a flash. He kicked off his boxers, and stepped into the tub.

Once he stood inside, the tub shrank. He was tall and big…six feet one inch of honed male muscle. Aroused male muscle, Avery noted with an awed, heart-stopping glance. Her nipples peaked. Her pulse picked up, and the air surrounding them became heavy with unspoken messages.

Perhaps this hadn't been such a good idea, after all.

But it was too late to undo the dare she'd instigated the moment she'd dropped that robe. If she told him she'd made a mistake, he'd laugh. Or accuse her of being a tease.

Her best choice was to tough it out. A few minutes of polite, uneasy silence, then she could chicken out with dignity, climb out the tub, say goodnight, and that would be that.

Avery sank lower into the water, and shut her eyes.

Except it wasn't quite that easy.

Images of his naked form warmed by soft candle flame danced across her eyelids. The smooth golden skin. The sculpted muscles. His burgeoning erection...

This was how she was getting over the man?

She bit back a gasp, and concentrated on mentally ranking the merlot wines she'd tasted today. She lost interest after rating the third wine. Ears straining, she tried to figure out what he was doing.

Was he looking at her?

The silence throbbed like a writhing beast. Unwanted memories of the nights she'd spent in Guy's bed, making love, entwined her. Now he was naked, a foot away from her, probably eating her alive with his eyes.

Avery couldn't breathe.

She knew she had to exorcise him. Forever.

"Did you get a chance to make some notes for our presentation today?" When Guy finally broke the silence, she jumped, and wavelets lapped at her throat.

He wanted to talk business?

Avery cracked one eye open and sneaked a peek through the billowing steam. She didn't know whether to laugh or scream. Guy was lying back, his eyes closed, looking utterly relaxed. She'd steeled herself to resist him—tell him to go to hell—and the damn man was practically asleep.

And here she was back to being all knotted up, fully expecting him to leap on her!

Cheated.

It wasn't—couldn't possibly be—disappointment that crawled through her, could it? She was relieved that she didn't have to fight him off. Wasn't she?

Hmm. If she were absolutely, confidentially truthful she was a teensy-weensy bit miffed.

It made *no* sense.

"So did you?"

"Uh, yes. I made some notes."

Collecting her scattered wits, she tried to remember what the thrust of them had been. And gave up. While she'd been scrambling for her sanity, Guy had opened his eyes. His gaze locked with hers. Lord only knew what he'd seen in her eyes, because his mouth curved up into a slow, knowing smile.

"Miss me?"

"Today?" She tried to laugh it off as a joke. "I didn't get a chance. Especially since I used the few spare minutes I had to work out what we were going to say."

"Pity." Under the water his hand landed on her bare thigh.

A rush of emotion filled her. Desire. Confusion. Anger. All tangled up in a mass of contrary, conflicting feelings. Avery reminded herself of all the reasons why it was a bad idea to let this happen. For sure, she would get hurt again.

But her desperate caveats didn't help. His fingers trailed up…along her belly. Her breath caught as they skirted precariously close to the underside of her breast.

Guy Jarrod was a drug and her body craved its fix.

She knew she should be telling him "No".

Yet insanely when his fingers snagged hers, and tugged,

she allowed him to draw her through the bubbling water toward him.

"I thought about you."

Her insides melted. "I doubt it," she said snippily. "You had too much to do."

"Oh, I'm not talking about today—I'm talking about the past seven weeks."

At the admission, blood roared in her ears. Guy had kept count of time? Her resistance crumbled a little more.

"I keep remembering this…."

His fingers surrounded her nipple, and the little traitor hardened.

Guy groaned. His other arm came round her and he drew her close until her body slid over him breast-against-chest, her nipples brushing the water-sleek muscle under his skin.

"So responsive," he murmured into her ear, and shivers feathered down her spine. "How could I ever forget this?"

The hope plummeted.

It was the sex he'd thought about—not her.

A cold, dampening wave of disappointment swamped her. What had she expected? An avowal of love? For him it had always been all about sex, nothing else. Guy had no idea of the fantasies she'd woven around him.

Fantasies involving love…family…and forever after.

She must've been dreaming. Or drugged. By sex? Yet right now, sex was almost enough.

Sensation shuddered through her as his mouth closed on her tight nipple. Something close to ecstasy coursed through her blood, and she gave a moan of dark delight.

Nothing wrong with sex.

Especially since this time there'd be no emotional component. It would be nothing more than an exorcism of a very bad habit.

Her legs entwined with his. Breaking the connection of

his mouth on the tingling bud of flesh, Guy linked his hands behind her neck, and she again came into full, too-tantalizing contact with him. The softness of her breasts again brushed against his chest, and arousal spiraled. He pulled her head down, and she could no longer resist.

His tongue swept across her bottom lip. Lust surged through her when the tip of her tongue met his. He sucked it into his mouth, and then plundered the warm heat of her mouth, seeking out every corner.

His fingers explored the indent of her spine, then moved under her belly and slid between her legs. At the first intimate touch she stiffened reflexively, then her legs parted. She was twenty-seven years old, too old to fool herself that Guy could make all the silly, romantic dreams of love-for-life come true. She'd left those behind the night of her birthday.

She was a woman, not a girl.

With a woman's wants.

It was time to recognize that her desperation to find love was nothing more than a ticking biological clock—an animal need to find a mate to help her raise the brood of children she'd always yearned for.

The kiss ended. His touch did not. It was expert, knowing, and gave exactly what she craved. Opening her eyes, she saw that the taut mask of desire had transformed Guy's face. Not even candle glow could soften the hunger.

He wanted her.

She wanted him.

At least there was honesty in desire.

Tonight she'd settle for lust…and deal with the fallout tomorrow.

Stretching out a hand, her fingers lightly stroked the hard, bold length of him beneath the silken water.

Guy stopped caressing her, and used both hands to yank

her up. "Stop! If you do that it will all be over way too soon."

She gave him a wicked smile. "And we can't have that."

"No," he growled.

Avery bent forward and outlined his lips with the teasing tip of her tongue. His arms tightened around her, bringing her softness in contact with the hard rock-like ridge of his arousal. He raised his hips, and the friction was exquisite.

Another shift, and her body sheathed his.

His head went back, the tendons on his neck drew tight. Leaning forward, she tongued them, tasting the moisture of the water, the slight tang of salt from his skin.

He was moving below her, his body sliding within hers, heat twisting into a blaze of unbearable pleasure. The pressure built and built until her climax rushed toward her, at the same time as Guy shuddered beneath her.

Avery was floating on a cloud of pleasure.

Her skin was flushed a rosy shade, and her body was soft and pliant. She felt like she'd died and gone to heaven.

"So what about making this a more lasting arrangement?" Guy whispered, cupping her chin with his hand.

The dreamy, heavenly feeling evaporated. Her eyes popped open and, shocked, she gazed down into Guy's smiling eyes.

"A more lasting arrangement?"

Avery almost forgot to breathe. This was what she'd wanted…hoped for…those two toe-curling weeks in New York, before the rug had been ripped out from under her on the night of her birthday.

What was wrong with her? Did she want to marry a man who thought her easy, a conniving gold digger? A man who'd wanted to share her in a tryst with his friend?

The Guy she'd imagined herself in love with didn't exist.

"Marriage is a big decision," she said finally, slithering off him to sit beside him.

His hand fell away.

"I never meant marriage?" Guy's smile slipped. The intimacy between them widened into a chasm. "Don't make more out of it than it needs to be, Avery. There's no reason why we can't enjoy each other for as long as it lasts."

Avery's jaw dropped. This only demonstrated one more difference between them. A more lasting arrangement had different meanings to her and Guy. For him it hardly lasted past tomorrow…nothing more than hot sex with the gold-digging ex. For her it had meant a surge of hope.

Stupid.

Emotionally, Guy wasn't available. To be fair, he'd always made it clear that he wasn't in the market for a long-term relationship. She'd simply believed she could change his mind.

Her mistake.

Say no. Now!

Yet if she did say no, she'd always wonder…

What if…

No regrets.

Drowning herself in dead-end yearnings wasn't going to get her over the man. What had Matt said last night? *If you're going to live it up, pumpkin, Aspen is the place to do it. Indulge yourself.*

Avery bit her lip.

She didn't want to indulge herself with just any one…she wanted Guy. Her body wanted Guy. So why not give in? And get over him?

"So what do you think?" His hand brushed her leg under

the water. Clearly he'd decided she would go along with it. Her indignation flared up all over again.

Her good sense returned. "And what happens when the festival ends? When it's time for me to leave?"

He shrugged. "Does it matter? Let's take it one day—" his eyes grew slumberous "—and one night at a time."

Yes, an affair would suit him just perfectly.

"I'd want to think about that."

His look of surprise would've been comical if Avery had felt like laughing.

"I'm sure there's enough work in all the exclusive Aspen resorts and restaurants to keep you busy for a while. I'm sure I can help you secure some contracts."

"I'm sure you can," she muttered, her irritation with him escalating. Didn't he have any idea how that would look? People would take one look at her, at her obvious closeness to Guy and she'd be written off as a millionaire's paid-for mistress. The professional reputation she'd worked so hard to establish would be gone in a puff of smoke.

Of course, it was partially her own fault. She should never have fallen into his bed so quickly. But she'd been unable to resist him. She'd thought he was her soul mate.

Damn. Damn. Damn.

Discovering Guy still set her on fire would make it so easy to agree. She wasn't caving in so easily this time. She stood up and the water streamed off her. Conscious of Guy's smoldering gaze, she squared her shoulders. "I'm not sure I want to stay in Aspen."

"Why not? You know you want to." The corners of Guy's mouth curled up. He reached up and ran a finger down her leg until it came to rest in the hollow behind her knee. "I'm here."

His arrogant certainty took her breath away. She stepped away, over the lip of the hot tub. Picking up her terry robe she slid her arms into the sleeves and yanked the sash into a knot, then said brightly, "And so will I be—until the end of the month but I can't guarantee anything past that."

"Maybe by then the flame would have burned itself out."

She could only hope…

"Maybe," she agreed. "And maybe I'll be homesick for California."

"There's that, too." Reserve entered his tone and the slumberous warmth seeped out of his eyes. "Not even this kind of chemistry will survive the distance. In terms of my father's will, I have to stay in Aspen. So we'll only have the time you're here."

Lifting her shoulder, Avery let it fall carelessly. "Working with me every day, you'll have had enough of my company."

"I'm sure you're right." But Guy's expression was brooding.

So he wasn't happy about that? Good. Because she wouldn't concede more than she already had. Even though she was unbearably tempted to settle for the affair he offered.

Sashaying away from him took every bit of nerve she possessed. She tossed her reply over her shoulder. "I'll consider your offer. But don't hold your breath." He deserved to sweat.

Avery didn't know what she was going to decide. One part of her, the part full of defiant bravado, was dying to say yes…have glorious get-over-him sex and walk away, sated and smiling. Cured. The other more cautious part of her was terrified she'd be addicted for life.

And where would that leave her?

At the door, his voice arrested her. "Uh, I meant to ask. Any consequences?"

"Consequences?" She swung around and stared at him

blankly. He'd almost broken her heart. Did that count? Or did that only rank as mere collateral damage and therefore… inconsequential?

"Pregnancy," he said a trifle impatiently from the steaming tub as she continued to gaze at him.

Oh. "I'm not pregnant."

Thank heavens for that!

"Good." He gave her a thin smile. "That's one complication neither of us need at this stage of our lives."

Speak for yourself. But Avery knew better than to voice her soul-deep yearning for a child…a family. Guy would never understand.

The water swirled as he rose. Avery's eyes widened, but she forced herself not to look away from the sight of the water droplets running down his chest…over his flat, muscled stomach. Despite everything he'd done, she really did still want him. God. She was not going to survive this.

"I almost forgot. Art was going to come along to the first of the balloon landings tomorrow—we do a champagne breakfast on landing and I have some ideas for a new menu." Her breaking dismay must've shown on her face because Guy added with a mocking smile, "You don't need to come if you don't want."

How early could it be?

"I'll be there," she said, pursing her mouth. "What time?"

"The ascent is at dawn." His grin deepened at her horrified groan. "I haven't forgotten you're not a morning person. Dress for comfort—jeans, boots and a jacket work best."

In one bound he was over the edge of the hot tub. Avery didn't wait another second, she fled.

Five

To Guy's surprise Avery was already waiting in the lobby early on Sunday morning, studying the framed photos of the celebrity guests that had been taken every season since the resort opened.

She must've sensed him because she swung around at his approach. To his surprise, the Avery who peered at him resembled a sleepy, fluffy owl rather than the svelte, petite doll he was more accustomed to. She was even wearing spectacles—something he'd never seen her don in daylight.

At his curious look, she said, "I didn't get enough sleep for my contact lenses to be comfortable. I'll put them in later."

"You don't need them."

He suspected she'd suffered lack of sleep for the same reason as he had. That quick coupling in the spa hadn't been nearly enough; he'd wanted her in his bed, all night long. Lust bolted through him. Just in time he stopped himself from babbling that she looked just as beautiful with glasses as without.

Not flattery, but true, he realized with a slight sense of shock as he inspected her.

Wearing figure-hugging white jeans and a cropped denim jacket, she glowed with vitality. The glasses simply added a scholarly twist to the sexy package. The hint of studious, good girl added by the glasses only served to accentuate the simmering sexuality that her pouty mouth and curvaceous body radiated.

To his relief, the group booked to go ballooning trooped into the lobby, providing a much-needed distraction from just how much of his thoughts Avery consumed. But not before Guy took in the appreciative smile one of the men bestowed on her. A sharp pang of annoyance caused him to turn away, before he snarled at a guest of the resort.

Hot damn but he had it bad.

Shoving his hands into his jeans' pockets, Guy hunched his shoulders and headed through the open, double glass doors, past the sleepy doorman in blue-and-gold livery, and out into the crisp, cool dawn air. Autumn was not yet here, but soon it would be.

To one side of the Manor Lodge, on a wide concrete apron that doubled as a helipad, he made out the figures of three pilots and a few members of the chase crew tending to the colorful nylon envelopes spread out on the concrete, while wicker baskets waited for passengers. The rest of the chase crew, including the resort staff who would be attending to the state-of-the-art catering, stood around joking and chatting and drinking coffee from paper cups.

An engine-driven fan droned to life and the red envelope of the closest balloon began to inflate. Minutes later the burners started to hiss, heating the cold air, and the envelopes rose above the baskets amidst whoops of delight from the guests. Twenty-odd guests quickly sorted themselves into three groups and entered the baskets to pose for last-minute photos and wave to well-wishers.

Once the first balloon started to ascend, the others swiftly followed.

"Isn't that simply stunning?"

Avery spoke from behind Guy as fingers of sunlight poked over the mountain ridge behind them and caressed the vivid balloons with morning light, brightening the dawn sky to a blaze of red, magenta and yellow.

Guy turned. The blue of her eyes was blinding, and her smile caused a fresh rush of heat. He swallowed. "You can go up one morning if you want," he said, his voice sounding hoarse even to his own ears.

She shook her head. "Never in a million years. I'm afraid of heights."

"You?" Guy gave a choke of laughter. "I can't imagine you afraid of anything."

Although Avery might be delicate and fine-boned, she could be as fierce and fiery as a tigress with cubs. That thought caused him to grin—because Avery was the least maternal woman he'd ever met. It had been a major reason for his attraction to her back in New York. She was so focused on her career—which suited him just fine. He'd made a habit of steering clear of starry-eyed women with marriage written all over them in diamond-bright letters.

"I get dizzy," she said with clear regret. "So you'll never catch me up there."

"In a balloon you don't get that vertigo feeling."

"Oh, sure."

"Really! The ride is smoother than I can ever describe. You move with the wind. No swaying or jostling. So never say never."

"Forget it, Guy!"

"Sometimes one needs to take risks, walk a little on the wild side."

She took a step away from him and wrapped her arms around her stomach. "I've done some dumb things in my life, but this sounds too wild for me."

Her face had closed up.

Was she talking about sleeping with Jeff…or what had happened last night between them? He had no intention of discussing Jeff—the anger hadn't yet settled. "I never pegged you for a 'fraidy cat,'" he taunted gently in an effort to bridge the chasm that suddenly yawned between them.

"Too bad. You're not talking me into this." She hunched her shoulders. "I'm too risk-averse."

Risk-averse? Avery? Puzzled, he frowned at her. "Not sure I swallow that."

She glowered at him. "Because I leapt into bed with you the first day we met? Not my smartest move, I'll admit. It's contaminated everything you think about me."

Did she count their affair as one of the dumb mistakes she'd made? That offended him.

"Contaminated? Hardly!" He moved closer to her, and lowered his voice to a husky growl. "Hey, let me tell you, there was nothing wrong with what we did together in New York. It was one of the most memorable times of my life. And last night was pretty damned amazing, too."

He wasn't lying.

He'd missed her, dammit.

Laying a hand along her cheek, he cupped it in his palm. "You're so honest in bed, there's none of the pretence women often play at."

For a moment he thought she was going to fling herself into his arms. There was a luminous expression in her eyes that made his chest tighten in a way that was new…and more than a little disconcerting.

She started to say something, then she pulled away. "Not here, Guy, we're in public."

Annoyance jabbed him at her stubborn insistence to keep him at a distance. "Are you too scared to let anyone know that we're—" he searched for a word to describe the scorching electricity they shared "—lovers?"

She snorted. "Lovers? That implies an intimacy we don't share."

Her dismissal was like a burr beneath a quarterhorse's tail. "Nothing wrong with the pleasure we've shared. And which we could continue to share." If she stopped being so darned pigheaded. But he didn't add that.

Nor did he point out that for someone as risk-averse as Avery claimed to be they'd taken a hell of a risk last night. It had been out of character for him—not because he feared risks, but because he took responsibility for his actions. All his actions. Last night was the first time in his life that he'd had sex without a condom—he'd never done that even in his most reckless teen years.

While he knew from their past that Avery protected herself against pregnancy, he'd risked his own health.

It wouldn't happen again. Ever. He didn't need the kind of consequences that might flow from such spur-of-the-moment stupidity.

But damn, it had been good....

Instead of looking at him, she tipped her head back. The early morning sun turned the ends of her eyelashes to gold. "I don't need to experience life from up there," she said, changing the subject. "I can do it perfectly well with both feet on the ground."

"Then you'll never see the fields rolling out under you, never touch the leaves on the treetops, nor see the elk grazing on the mountaintops—and that's losing out as far as I'm concerned." From the set of her chin, he could see he didn't appear to be getting anywhere. "If you tried it, you might find it worth it. The view is fantastic from up there—a whole different perspective. You can see for miles in every direction."

"Sounds like you enjoy it."

"I go every year during the festival." Except that wasn't true. Not anymore. "At least, I used to take a ride every year," he amended. "I haven't been home for a while."

At last she looked at him, her scrutiny intense, making him shift uncomfortably.

"I was busy." The unspoken question in her eyes caused him to prevaricate. "Come on, the chase crews are on the move."

Striding across the concrete, he reached in his jeans' pocket for the keys to a black SUV with the name Jarrod Ridge emblazoned on the side. Once they were both inside he started the vehicle and pulled in behind the second minivan that contained the catering crew.

Avery was perched on the edge of her seat. The tight lines had left her mouth and he could sense her rising excitement. "Is the landing spot pre-arranged?"

Guy laughed. "If only! The crew in the first vehicle are in radio contact with the pilots and have a rough idea where the balloons will come down. But it's never exact because the pilots are at the mercy of the winds."

She snorted. "And that's supposed to reassure me about going up there?"

"The pilots are very experienced—they're also in touch with air traffic control at the local airport."

Avery fell silent for a few minutes. When she spoke again it was to sigh and say, "It is beautiful out here."

Guy had to agree. The sun was rising quickly, illuminating the meadows in the valley and the jutting mountain peaks.

"Just wait a few weeks until fall arrives and the aspens turn gold—it's spectacular."

"I'll be gone by then."

Not if he had anything to do with it. Avery owed him—and he wasn't going to let her go until he was good and ready.

"We'll see," he growled. "I'm still holding my breath."

There was an uneasy pause.

Finally Avery broke it. "You clearly love it here. What kept you from returning all those years?"

So she intended to avoid the tension that bristled between them? Guy was itching for a confrontation…one that might explode into passion. Make her say yes. Maybe her course was wisest. For now.

Keeping his focus on the road, he said in the most even voice he could muster, "Work. After leaving school I studied haute cuisine in France, then worked for several years in London, before returning to the States to open Baratin. There wasn't time to come to Aspen."

"'The finest French restaurant on the east coast'. Or at least that's what *Cuisine* magazine called it."

The accolades didn't ease Guy's guilt. "This past month was the longest I've spent home in almost two decades."

Home, funny that he still thought of Jarrod Ridge as home. Yet he'd only returned because of the terms of his father's will. If he and his brothers and sisters didn't stay, they would lose out on their inheritance.

None of them were ready to forfeit that.

Her hand brushed his leg, hovered, then settled on his thigh. Oh, hell. His muscles clenched involuntarily under the tantalizing pressure of her fingertips.

"Guy, your father knew you loved him."

Her words wiped out the pleasure her touch had bestowed. Unerringly, she'd honed in on the crux of his guilt and pain. "Did he? I'm not so sure."

"You saw him before he died?"

"I was too late."

And not for the first time.

He couldn't stand to see the pity in Avery's eyes. God help him if she saw all the way to his soul and the festering regret.

If only...

"But you spoke to him while we were—" she hesitated "—together. I even took a message for you to call your dad." She sounded rueful. "You know what? I never even realized I was talking to the legendary Donald Jarrod."

Just as well.

Otherwise he might never have discovered that all Avery wanted was a man made of gold. She would've taken care to hide her avaricious streak from him, would never have gone after Jeff. He didn't voice the cynical thought. Instead he swung the SUV left into a lane lined with poplars.

"I saw my father not long before I met you. He came to New York." Because Guy had refused to go to Aspen. "He wanted me to take over running all the bars and restaurants at Jarrod Ridge." He gave a crooked smile. "I refused. Then he died. Now I'm doing what he asked, anyway."

"And you wish you'd told him yes while he was alive."

Bull's eye.

Guy swung the wheel, pulling the SUV onto the shoulder of the road, then turned in his seat to face her.

The understanding and empathy that glimmered in her eyes nearly undid him. He forced out a shuddering breath, and a heartbeat later he hauled her into his arms.

"Your father knows you loved him," she murmured against his parka.

That uncertainty lay at the root of Guy's guilt. He'd resisted all his father's calls to return. Deep down he'd blamed his father for driving them apart after his mother's death. "I doubt it—even though I tell myself that one day we'll meet again, I'm not even sure that I believe that either. But thanks."

With a sigh, he set her away from him.

Then, narrowing his gaze until he located the minivans in the distance, he put the SUV back into gear and trod on the gas to close the gap.

"Guy, my parents died in a boating accident when I was a two-year-old."

"I didn't know that." She'd never told him that—he wondered what other vital, formative information she'd withheld.

"Uncle Art used to tell me I carried them with me, in my heart. They were with me all the time. But that worried me—I didn't want them in my heart, I wanted to know they were up there." Avery pointed through the windshield to the blue sky overhead. "It's so perfect, so blue, so clear. How could there not be heaven and angels? I used to tell Uncle Art that one day I'd go there to visit them."

So she still believed in angels and ever-after. How'd he missed this softer, more idealistic side to her? Guy wondered what other illusions she still clung to. "You wanted to visit them up there even though you're scared of heights?"

A quick sideways glance revealed her smile and the dimple in her cheek. "You know, I never gave that a thought—I told my Aunt I could catch a plane from LAX."

Guy couldn't help himself, he gave a shout of laughter.

High above where the balloons floated sunrays glinted off a plane. "Matt is somewhere up there," Avery said suddenly.

He sobered. "Matt?"

"My cousin." There was an odd note in her voice. "You've seen him."

He couldn't remember meeting her cousin. One thing his father's death had brought home was it was often better to say nothing than to mouth an inane bunch of platitudes at someone's loss. First her parents, then her cousin, Matt. He decided to keep it factual.

"I don't remember meeting him. Was it in New York?"

"No, last night. In the sky lounge."

Confused, he slowed and turned his head to stare at her.

"Dark hair. Tall." She held her hand above her head, almost touching the roof of the SUV. "We shared a drink. You came in. And left before I could introduce you. He was at the champagne-and-oyster party the previous night, too. He flew home today."

Her cousin. He switched his attention back to the road. The man who'd hugged her...was her cousin Matt.

Not dead.

And not her lover.

Guy felt himself flush. After a moment of feeling like a complete idiot, he laughed. "You should have told me."

"And ruined your fun?"

The agony of emotion that had stabbed him when she'd embraced Matt last night had been anything but funny.

"Not nice," he said reprovingly.

Avery sounded unrepentant. "Serves you right for jumping to conclusions."

"When you said he was up there, I thought you meant he was dead. Like my father."

He nosed the SUV through an open gate into a field and came to a stop beside the chase vehicles. By the time he got to the passenger door, Avery was already on the ground.

"Guy—" she touched his arm "—I'm so sorry."

Guy wished he'd kept his mouth shut. He didn't want her feeling pity for him. He wanted her teasing humor back. Everyone had been pussyfooting around the family since his father's death almost six weeks ago.

"There's a lot to do," he said gruffly. "And almost two dozen hungry people who have just come off the high of a lifetime to feed."

Guy was right. It was hectic.

After the balloonists landed the pilots shepherded them together for a celebration ceremony. Avery was conscious of the wonder on the faces of the new initiates, but there was no time to watch the ceremony as Guy and members of the Jarrod Ridge catering crew whipped up a scrumptious gourmet breakfast.

Mimosas—the orange juice and champagne fizzing in tall glasses, slices of melon, eggs Benedict, and bagels with smoked salmon and cream cheese were among the delicacies spread out on the tables that had been set up and laid with white linen and gleaming silver cutlery.

"How artistic it looks." Avery stood back to admire the effect. "I don't know why you think the menu needs overhauling. It's perfect."

"Delicious, too, I hope."

She laughed at Guy's droll comment. "That's a given. Food always tastes better outdoors."

"That so?"

She nodded emphatically. "Definitely so."

"We'll have to test that theory out sometime."

The first of the balloonists arrived at the tables, their faces glowing with excitement and their hair windblown.

"But not now," Guy added, as he moved to stand behind where the serving tables were set up.

A tall Canadian loaded up his plate and paused beside Avery. "Where are you sitting?"

Avery smiled at him. He'd greeted her back in the lobby. He had a friendly grin and appeared popular with the group. "I'm only—"

Before she could complete the sentence and tell him she was part of the resort's crew, Guy spoke from behind her, "Avery is with me."

The heavy-handed male warning was enough to make Avery see red.

Six

Avery stalked away from Guy, and found herself saying, "Is there space at your table?"

The Canadian, whose name turned out to be Todd, introduced her to his group of friends and they all started to rave about how awesome the flight had been. But Avery found it hard to concentrate.

All she was aware of was Guy's smoldering presence at the next table.

Why did she care? He had no right to behave like a complete idiot over Todd. She and Guy weren't even a couple, darn it. He'd been the one who'd always made sure she tendered no hopes in that direction.

She had a job to do and she would do it. She wasn't about to let Uncle Art down. Nor was she going to put up with Guy's arrogance.

Avery speared a piece of melon and chewed.

At the back of her mind she was conscious that she wasn't

being totally fair on Guy. She'd allowed him to provoke her into saying and doing utterly stupid things—because he infuriated her.

You're so honest in bed, he'd said on their way here, *there's none of the pretence women often play at.*

If only he knew...

Instead of grasping the opportunity to admit how she'd misled him about Jeff, she'd chickened out.

Maybe she was the 'fraidy cat Guy had called her. It was impossible to explain what had driven her to imply that she'd slept with Jeff. It had been such a stupid thing to do—heck, she didn't even understand the foolish impulse herself.

Draining the hot, aromatic coffee, she set the empty cup down on the table.

All she knew was that she'd wanted to hurt him as he'd hurt her with his belief that she was an easy little gold digger. But that was no excuse. When she'd discovered he'd never pimped her to Jeff she should have cleared up the misunderstanding then and there. Instead, she'd discovered a deep yearning for him to trust her unreservedly. When Guy had eyed her with disgust, she'd lost all sense.

And the damage had been done.

Oh, what a tangled web.

Now he had her back up with his dog-in-the-manger attitude about Todd. Again she'd instantly reacted, rebelling against his dark, thunderous glare. And proceeded to dig herself deeper into the mess she'd created.

What did Guy think she was going to do, in heaven's name? Sleep with Todd?

The frustration and anger cut deep.

Guy didn't trust her.

At the heart of it all, that was what hurt most. That was what made her act so perversely. Her disappointment at his lack of trust about Jeff...then Matt...and now Todd. God, she'd just told him he'd been wrong about Matt, but did he learn? No, he simply leapt to the next wild conclusion about her.

If he knew her at all, Guy would never have believed her capable of that kind of betrayal. If he'd known anything about her he would've found it impossible to believe. She was really quite proper in her way. Not a wild wanton at all. But he hadn't cared to find out who she was. All he was interested in was a sexy body in his bed. Coupled with his distrust, that made her loath to tell him about her stupidity.

Yet despite her annoyance with Guy she found herself tasting the food and observing the guests and keeping mental notes about what they ate and what they pushed away.

Still annoyed an hour later, Avery escaped the ride back with Guy by hopping in one of the other resort minivans with the balloonists on the way back. But when they pulled up in the courtyard, Guy was waiting for her, his eyes still stormy.

"I'll introduce you to Louis Leclere, the chef at Chagall's."

"I met him yesterday, at one of the talks I listened to," Avery said. "He told me that you and he are old friends."

The Frenchman had confessed that Guy had lured him to Jarrod Ridge just over a month ago.

Guy's mouth tightened. "Let me introduce you to the resort's head barman then."

"Oh, I met him, too. Louis thoughtfully introduced us. In fact the three of us are meeting—" she glanced at her watch "—in thirty minutes. They're going to show me around the cellars. I better go change into something more suitable." She gestured to the dust on the hem of her white jeans. "Otherwise I'll be late."

"Avery," Guy put a restraining hand on her arm, and

glanced meaningfully at Todd who was hovering nearby, "Louis tends to have a devastating effect on women. We have a policy that staff don't date guests—I've told him that already. But I wouldn't want you to tempt him to break the rules."

Angrily, she shook off his hand. "Well, since I'm neither a guest nor staff but an independent contractor, that shouldn't affect me. Of course, that won't affect me asking Louis out on a date—he's staff, and I've always had a thing for French accents."

Guy glowered.

Jerk.

Avery spent the rest of the day avoiding Guy. Until he finally cornered her late that afternoon in the Sky Lounge where she was studying the proposed drink list for the winter ski season and jotting down notes into a moleskin notebook.

"I shouldn't have said what I did this morning about staff and guest liaisons," he said abruptly halting beside the bar counter.

"No, you shouldn't," she agreed, gazing unseeingly at the list in front of her. "You should've trusted me to behave with professionalism."

Her rebuke was met with silence.

"Truce?" he said at last.

He had a long way to go. Setting the list down with a snap, Avery glanced up to find that Guy's confusion was written over every hard line on his face. "If you're not prepared to trust me, then so long as you treat me with the respect you accord other employees and contractors we have a truce."

Heat flared in his eyes, turning them a smoldering, smoky gray. "Impossible. I can't treat you like I treat everyone else. We're lovers."

"Shh!"

Avery glanced around to see if he'd been overheard. But the nearest group, three young women and two men, were clustered around the bar counter sipping margaritas and flirting furiously, showing no interest in her and Guy.

"Not any more."

"But we were. We will be again. Soon."

He brushed his fingers across her cheek and she flinched away. He couldn't help remembering how demonstrative Avery had been in New York, always ready to touch him, stroke him. With the exception of last night, all she'd seemed to have done since she came to Jarrod Ridge was back away from him.

"I don't want people knowing we had a relationship."

That made it sound like she had no intention of considering his suggestion that they enter a more lasting arrangement during her stay.

He drew a deep breath. He wasn't going to accept that. They were not through yet. No woman walked out on him. "Avery, it's nothing to be ashamed of."

"Not for you. Everyone will just think 'what a stud', while I get the sniggers."

"It won't be like that." Guy raked his hand through his hair, but the dark, shaggy strands sprang stubbornly back.

After a pause during which her blue eyes dueled with his night-gray ones, he said, "Tell you what, let's have dinner at Chagall's tonight."

Avery shook her head. "Can't you understand? I don't want to be seen out with you, Guy."

"We need to talk more about what you'll be doing at Jarrod Ridge over the next few weeks."

Avery had been dying to sample the dishes at the resort's premier restaurant. But she got the feeling that dinner was less about setting up a professional work relationship than trying to get her back into his bed.

Why was he bothering to pursue her? It wasn't about her agreement to step into Uncle Art's shoes. Guy had been averse to that from the start, and he could easily contract another sommelier. Nor did she flatter herself that he wanted only her in his bed. He'd made his opinion of her clear. Finding another lover would be equally easy for a man like Guy. It had surprised her that he hadn't already acquired a new lover, until she'd realized that his father's death and the terms of his will had left Guy with no time to find a new girlfriend. How fortuitous for him that she'd turned up, saving him the bother.

No, the only attraction she held was the fact that she wasn't falling over herself to get back into his bed. How galling that must be when he'd already labeled her easy and a gold digger….

With a jolt she took in Guy looking at her expectantly, no doubt waiting for her to agree to dinner—and to serve herself up as dessert.

"No thanks, not tonight. It's been a long day, and I need a good night's sleep. Alone," she added pointedly.

By the tight line of his lips she knew he'd gotten the message.

"Then I won't be seeing you for a few days," he said. "One of the national supermarket chains is interested in stocking Go Green products, and Jeff and I are meeting with them in New York to hammer out an agreement."

Avery forced herself not to react to the mention of Jeff-the-Jerk's name. What would it help? It wouldn't repair the damage she and Jeff between them had done or encourage Guy to trust her. He'd made it more than clear that his loyalty lay with Jeff, and the friendship and business relationship they shared.

All she said was, "Well, I hope your meeting is productive."

"No reason why it shouldn't be. Oh, and speaking of meetings," he added, "on the afternoon I get back we'll be having a progress briefing about the Food and Wine Gala before Blake flies out back to New York. You should be there." Guy pointed to her notebook. "Some of the information you've collected will be very useful."

By Thursday morning, Avery had convinced herself that she didn't care if Guy's loyalty lay with Jeff. All she wanted was a professional relationship with a man she'd been dumb enough to almost fall in love with. Her notebook clutched in her hand, she scanned the family room on the top floor of Jarrod Manor with interest. Forcing herself to ignore the impact that seeing Guy again had on her, she inspected the high beams, the woven rugs scattered over the landing, the wood finish that all combined to give a cozy, homey feel.

The Jarrods were seated around a sunken conversation pit in front of a fireplace, which in winter would give the room a warm ambience.

Blake patted the table to get everyone's attention. The group slowly fell silent. "Gavin…Trevor…you're both here. Anyone missing?"

Gavin and Trevor were remarkably similar-looking in coloring and build and even mood, Avery noticed. Much more so than Blake and Guy. She compared the twins. Their dark hair and determined jawlines were the only resemblance they shared.

"Except Melissa," said Erica from an armchair set to one side. "She was feeling off color and went home."

"She's been tired a lot lately," said Christian, Erica's fiancé, who was perched on the arm of her chair. "Perhaps she should go see a doctor."

Guy shuffled a pile of papers. "Okay, let's get down to business."

Nothing could've more effectively made Avery realize how wrong he was for her. All he cared about was business...and sex.

Even his sister's health was of little concern to him.

Nothing about him made him a good prospect for the husband she wanted, for the father of the family she yearned for. So why had she wasted three whole days pining after the darn man?

He didn't want a family. Look how relieved he'd been when she'd told him there had been no consequences to their affair. If she'd had any sense she might've told him about the very light period she'd had and made him fret a little.

In fact, it was probably worth purchasing a pregnancy test just to make sure there'd been no slip. Not that she expected there to be a baby, but the two weeks she'd spent in Guy's bed in New York had been over her most fertile time of the month. She'd been on the Pill then, even though she was off it now.

She doodled on the pad on front of her. A row of daisies with smiling faces. She told herself that it was for the best that she couldn't have conceived. That she should be as happy as the daisies she'd captured on the legal pad.

After the meeting was over she'd go into town. Just to make sure.

Guy couldn't find Avery anywhere.

He'd unexpectedly missed her in the days he'd been gone, and now she'd vanished into thin air.

Rita confirmed Avery wasn't booked for a treatment in the spa. Nor had Louis seen her all morning—much as it galled him to ask his friend if he'd seen her. So she hadn't been to

Chagall's. Reception said she hadn't used her card to access her room.

He was dying to tell her about the success he'd had with Go Green. Jeff hadn't made the meeting in the end, and Guy had been left to do all the wheeling and dealing alone. It was the first time that Jeff had let him down, and Guy knew it could only be because his partner still felt awkward about having slept with Avery. The relationship between them had become strained.

Despite Jeff's absence, the supermarket chain had placed a large order, but there were tough deadlines and production would have to get moving. Now Guy found himself wanting to watch Avery tip her head to one side as she evaluated the progress he'd made, to hear her arguments against it. And watch her eyes widen and her head bob if she considered the opportunity as good as he did.

So where the hell was she?

Grumpily, Guy took his cell phone out from the chest pocket of his white business shirt and located her number. Three rings later her breathy voice greeted him. Instantly desire curled in his groin.

"Where are you?" he asked more brusquely than he'd intended.

"In town."

She'd gone to town? Why? "You didn't tell me you were going."

"You didn't ask."

"Why the big secret?"

"It's not a secret."

A chill feathered along his spine at the defensive note in her voice. Avery was not being completely truthful with him. *Why?*

What was she hiding?

Was she meeting someone—hell, be honest—he wanted

to know if she was meeting Todd. He swallowed the bile in the back of his throat. Had they become an item in his absence?

Guy suspected he was being unreasonable…he'd never reacted with this kind of unwarranted jealousy with his other girlfriends. But then he'd never experienced this degree of turmoil over any of them.

"I wanted to talk to you," he said finally.

"What about?"

Suddenly it all felt flat. This call wasn't going the way he'd planned. "It doesn't matter."

"We can talk when I get back—sorry, I have to go now,"

Guy stared at his BlackBerry in disbelief. She'd killed the call. No woman ended a call until *he* was good and ready…it was always he who cut the woman short. In New York Avery had been openly admiring, now she barely had time for him. He didn't like the role reversal one little bit.

But why the hell did it matter?

He didn't want her to love him. The last thing he wanted was a needy woman—he'd made it his life's mission to avoid them. All he wanted was sex. Good sex. No, he wanted more, he wanted great sex. The kind of sex he'd always had with Avery.

But that didn't explain this sudden pressing need to talk to her about how the Go Green meetings had gone.

Guy shook his head, confused.

The sooner he got Avery back into his bed the better. In his experience sex fixed everything.

Seven

Back in her hotel room, Avery stood in the bathroom and stared at the applicator stick.

The emotion that surged through her at the sight of the single pink line was not the relief she'd expected. Instead she felt unaccountably sad.

Her throat was tight and achy. She wanted to cry.

There'd been two tests in the box she'd driven to Aspen to buy earlier. Both had given the same result.

One pink line.

Not pregnant.

It's for the best, she tried to convince herself. It was what Guy had wanted. What she should've wanted, too. If she'd had any sense.

She ought to be dancing around with delighted relief. Not staring at the second stick praying for the second pink line to appear.

Because she wanted a baby. She longed for a family.

And, damn it, she wanted Guy, too. All in the same breath. Even though she knew such pie-in-the-sky dreams were utterly impossible.

Pink. She felt downright blue.

A knock sounded on the door of her room.

Avery stuck the traitorous stick back into the box and hurried out of the bathroom.

Wrenching the door open she found Guy on the other side.

Horrors. For a moment she couldn't marshal her thoughts. All she could think of was the telltale pregnancy test sitting on the bathroom slab, incriminating evidence of all her dashed hopes.

"Aren't you going to invite me in?"

"Wh-what are you doing here?" she stuttered. For a wild moment she considered slamming the door in his face.

"I came to help you move your stuff."

"Move my stuff?" She retreated into the room, and barely noticed that he'd followed.

"Didn't Reception call? I've changed your room." He frowned as he scanned it. "I didn't know you were given a room in this wing. The view isn't great."

"It doesn't matter—I spend so little time here. Frankly, I'd be grateful for a broom cupboard, I know how scarce accommodation in Aspen is."

"Now's not too bad, but during the ski season it's diabolical."

She didn't bother to remind him she wouldn't be here for the ski season.

He strode across the room.

"Where are you going?" she squawked, intent on distracting him before he entered the bathroom and discovered the telltale stick. She'd already told him she wasn't pregnant, she didn't want him doubting her.

Instead he stopped just to the left of the door to the bathroom, and threw open the wardrobe doors.

Avery's breath whooshed out in a gust of relief.

He spoke into the wardrobe. "It shouldn't take you long to pack up."

"I'm not packing up."

"If you don't want to move into another room, you can move in with me. Because you never did give me an answer. And I've been very patient, I've given you more time than you need."

She stared at his back, achingly conscious of the shaggy length of his hair where it brushed the collar of his T-shirt.

"I'm not moving into your quarters."

"The view is far better from my suite upstairs."

She wished she could see his face. "I'm sure it is. But as I just said, I'm not in my room enough for it to matter."

He spun away from the wardrobe.

Avery caught a glimpse of tumult in the dark gray eyes, before his jaw firmed, and he moved toward her with long, swinging strides.

Hooking his arms around her shoulders, he bent his head until his forehead touched her hair.

"I want you with me," he said into the cave of space between them.

Oh, dear heaven. How was she supposed to resist this?

If only he'd been a different kind of man...

A family man.

But he wasn't. And she had to be strong. She had to resist.

"I'm not going to have an affair with you."

"And I'm not going to accept no for an answer."

Her breath whooshed out in frustration. "You have to accept it. You can't force me to move in with you."

"I can certainly use every advantage I have to persuade you." His lips brushed hers in a light teasing kiss.

"I need some space," she said desperately.

"Why? Just admit you want me." He kissed her again, his mouth lingering on hers.

Unfair!

"We're working together. Trying to keep a professional distance." Her breath mingled with his. "We're both going to need space, time away from each other. Otherwise we'll drive each other crazy." And she refused to let herself fall in love with him all over again.

"I don't want any space between us…." He pulled her up against his body. "Almost a week has already slipped away, I want to spend every remaining minute we have together."

He sunk his tongue into her mouth in a primitive act of possession that sent a thrill of desire along Avery's bloodstream.

The sentiment was all well and good, but Avery knew he didn't mean it. Not in the way that she needed him to mean it. All he was talking about was sex.

He wanted her within reach all night long.

And first thing in the morning, if it came to it.

Guy was a demanding lover. He'd take whatever she gave, without giving much of himself in return. Having her in his bed, at his convenience, didn't mean he wanted to be close to her.

Not in any of the ways that really mattered.

Avery drew away. "No. I'm keeping my stuff in my room. This room. I'm not your lover anymore. I don't want special treatment. I don't want the staff, your family, thinking that I am your lover."

His hand brushed her hair off her face, his touch so gentle her throat thickened. "I'm not going to give up until you agree."

She was going to have to spell it out this time. So that he'd understand and never ask again. She couldn't bear this.

"Because I've worked damn hard to get where I am. And I'm not having anyone denigrating my efforts by saying that I got there because I slept with one of the Almighty Jarrods."

"That didn't matter to you in New York."

"Because I didn't know you were a Jarrod then—not one of these Jarrods." She drew a steadying breath, refusing to be provoked. "And in New York I didn't know anyone—I was on temporary assignment. Here, at the Food and Wine Gala, there are a lot of people I know. People who respect me. People who may offer me work."

She tilted her head back and gazed up at him.

"How long do you think their respect will last once they know I'm living in your penthouse suite?"

"It won't be like that."

"It's always like that. Everyone will think me a lucky little gold digger who landed a rich lover—exactly what you accused me of only a few days ago."

His gaze fell before hers.

"I apologize, I shouldn't have said that."

"No, you shouldn't. Your apology is accepted. But it doesn't change the fact that I'm not moving in with you."

There was a long pause. Avery tensed, waiting for an argument, for him to sweep her up in his arms, for something.

But he only said, "We need to work on the presentation we're giving tomorrow."

Back to work. The professional relationship that was all she could ever afford to share with him.

So why did she want to sag with disappointment that he'd accepted her decision? At least she knew she could deal with Guy on the work front.

Hurriedly she said, "Well, we might as well talk about both presentations." The second presentation was next Wednesday, less than a week away. "Give me an hour, I'll come up to your suite." She made herself give him a cheeky smile. "Have dinner ready, but don't think that you can change my mind about staying the night."

Avery was true to her word.

The intercom buzzed exactly an hour later— and Guy activated the private elevator for her to come up, then opened the door to his suite.

She stepped into his living room, a tote slung over her shoulder and a bright smile on her face. She was wearing high-heel slides, a pair of her trademark white jeans and a strawberry-ice silk blouse that clung to her curves. She looked good enough to lick.

"Come in," said Guy huskily.

"Oh, that looks good."

Her attention had homed in on an array of mouthwatering tapas spread on the low square coffee table where two sofas sat beside the empty fireplace. "Funny how the sight of food always seems to remind me of how long it's been since I last ate."

"Room service," he said laconically.

She slid him an amused look as she sat down on the nearest sofa. "And there I thought you'd been slaving in the kitchen preparing our meal. You still owe me a meal—you promised to make me one in New York, and you never did."

Never again. He'd done that on the night of her birthday... and had been left cooling his heels while she entertained herself with Jeff.

"We've got a lot of work to get through," he said tersely. "Let's get started."

She didn't take the hint. "You know, while I stayed with you most of our food was take out from Baratin's—"

"What's wrong with that? Most women would kill to never have to cook."

"I cooked."

"Very occasionally—and then only breakfast." He tipped his head to the side. "Now that I think back, it was toast and cereal most mornings."

"Do you have any idea how intimidating it is to cook for a chef? Obviously not! Except you never cooked—I'm seriously beginning to wonder if you actually know how to cook, or whether you're just a fraud." She slanted him a teasing glance from under those fluttery eyelashes.

Despite the gloom that the memory of her birthday had cast over him, Guy found himself laughing. She'd always been able to charm a smile from him.

"Avery, that's something I sometimes wonder myself. I employ chefs these days. I seem to spend more time doing paperwork and juggling numbers than cooking. The business courses Dad insisted I take are being used more than my chef credentials."

"I'm always impressed when I watch food shows." She leaned back on the couch, folding her hands behind her head. With her glinting eyes half closed, she was all temptress. "Those so efficient chefs, chopping onions without weeping, producing masterpieces in minutes. You'll have to show me how it's done."

Guy suppressed the urge to rush to the kitchen, don an apron, anything to impress her. Been there, never again. "Maybe one day."

But he had no intention of exposing himself that way again.

Avery kicked off her slides. Guy caught a glimpse of pink-tipped toes before she tucked her feet underneath her. From her tote, she drew out a black notebook and a pen.

"Okay, so where shall we start?"

Guy was still admiring the picture she made, the way her white jeans clung to her thighs, and fantasizing about feeding her strawberries that he'd flambéed to impress her then licking the flavour from her lips.

Caught off guard by her businesslike demeanor he found himself stuttering, "Uh…I have a PowerPoint presentation that will provide some material."

She tipped her face toward the flat-screen television that dominated the wall across from where she sat, then looked expectantly back at him. "Let's watch it."

Hell, he hadn't linked his laptop.

Guy rubbed the back of his neck. "When we've finished talking."

She shifted, a little wriggle that had Guy clenching his teeth in frustration, before she settled again.

He barely knew what they talked about for the next twenty minutes, except that Avery seemed to take copious notes… and make numerous suggestions—none of which he was likely to retain.

Not when she was such a tempting distraction.

Finally, Avery closed her notebook with a snap and said, "Good, that should wrap it up."

Guy was simply relieved that the torture was at an end. Until she reached for a toothpick and speared a piece of spicy chorizo with it. Popping it in her mouth, she chewed, head tilted to one side, then said, "That was very tasty. There's a smoky flavor that would go well with an oaked and well-aged red made from tempranillo grapes."

"That would be a great match."

A frown furrowed her brow. "I detect a spice I can't place."

Guy tried to tell himself that this was still work. Matching food and wine. But his body refused to believe him. All he could do was stare at her mouth like a hungry hound after a meal.

"Have you eaten?"

He shook his head, not trusting his voice.

"You should."

With delicate grace she took a second toothpick out of the white porcelain holder and spiked a piece of chorizo then added a sun-dried tomato, and offered it to him.

His heart thumped.

He bent his head, took it from her fingers, aware of the unconscious eroticism of the gesture.

The sweetness of the tomato and the spicy sausage complemented one another.

"What do you think?" Her brow had crinkled. "Can you identify that elusive spice?"

"Pimentón," he said huskily, watching her help herself to a shrimp cake. "Spanish paprika."

She snapped her fingers. "You're right." Then she speared a fat, shiny black olive. "So," she said, "what thoughts do you have about the menus for the restaurants?"

This was work, what Jarrod Ridge was paying her for. No doubt she'd be keeping track of every second to bill the resort. He forced himself to concentrate. "A total re-vamp."

Another olive went the same way as the last. Guy almost growled. But he managed to feed himself and stanch some of the physical hunger. Too soon the platters on the table were empty.

"When are you going to put the PowerPoint on?"

She had to be joking, right?

One glance revealed she wasn't. The notebook was propped against her thigh, and a pencil twisted between her fingers. She expected them to work. Guy suppressed a sigh and hooked his laptop up to the flat screen. Then he settled down on the couch beside her.

He put his hand on her leg.

"Hey."

He took it off. This time he sighed loudly.

With no choice he focused on the screen, conscious of every move of her hand as she scribbled the occasional note.

The room grew darker. There were a couple of clips of interviews and Avery put her pad and pencil down on the coffee table.

"Seen enough?"

She shook her head. "I want to watch it all."

Guy's thoughts wandered. He'd seen parts of the presentation countless times. He was tempted to flick it forward, speed it up.

Dammit, he'd had enough of work.

He ached to kiss Avery. It had been too long. When her head brushed his shoulder, his pulse surged and he slung an arm around her. She rewarded him by snuggling up against him. Guy couldn't wait for the program to finish.

Her breathing grew more regular. Guy peered down at her through the dim light, and suppressed a groan.

Avery had fallen asleep!

She looked so young, so innocent, with her dark lashes falling against smooth cheeks. Guy stroked the feathery bangs off her face with gentle fingers. She stirred, and he stilled, but instead of waking she only burrowed closer.

Emotion bolted through him, fierce and primitive and defying him to put a name to it.

With one hand he pressed the remote and the screen went black. Scooping Avery up into his arms, he rose and headed for his bedroom. Muted light spilled from the bedside lamp. There, surrounded by the burgundy and muted gold décor, he laid her down and gently arranged the covers over her, before shedding his shirt, dropping his jeans and lowering himself beside her.

Instantly she curled into him.

The spontaneity of the gesture pierced his heart. Guy gathered her close, and closed his eyes. Nuzzling at the soft fluff of her hair he was conscious of a welcome sense of contentment seeping through him.

This time he wasn't going to let her go.

She woke in an unfamiliar room.

Avery blinked against the shaded glow of the bedside lamp. Shifting, she became aware of the warmth of a body in the bed beside her. Guy! They'd been in the sitting room of his suite, she'd felt replete and pleasantly tired. Then nothing...

They hadn't made love. She would've remembered that.

Her body was curved into Guy's spoon-fashion, her legs tangled with his. She suspected his were bare—unlike hers that were still clad in jeans.

At least he hadn't undressed her.

He'd retained that much decency.

Nor had he made love to her.

Okay, so what did that prove? Only that Guy wasn't a necrophiliac. She stifled a giggle and eased herself away from him. He groaned and rolled onto his back.

Avery slipped quickly out the king-size bed, her bare feet sinking into thick carpet. Guy's arm was flung out above his head, his dark hair mussed. In sleep he looked younger, carefree, more like the Guy she'd met...what?...could it be only ten weeks ago now? She couldn't remember what her life had been like before Guy.

A sigh escaped. Once the Food and Wine Gala ended, so would her time with Guy.

For a moment she contemplated diving back into the soft, welcoming bed and cozying up to him. They could make love. Add another treasured memory to the trove in her heart to take away with her when she left. Then she squared her shoulders.

She wasn't going to spend the night with Guy…and have the world know about it. She wasn't going to become his lover—at least not until he began to trust her. Really trust her.

Far better to sneak out like a thief in the night now than to face that humiliation in the morning when the staff came on duty.

Swinging about, Avery headed into the darkened sitting room to find her shoes, her notebook and her tote, before she risked her self-respect.

Guy stirred, and reached out an arm…only to discover an expanse of smooth sheet. An empty expanse. His eyes shot open, and he rolled over.

The bed was cool, no residue of body warmth lingered. The only signs that Avery had been there were the slight indent on the pillow beside him and the lingering scent of her perfume.

Despite Avery saying that she would not move into his suite, Guy had comfortably expected to be able to change her mind last night—once he got her there. He hadn't banked on her falling asleep, but he'd certainly expected her to still be in his bed when he wakened. Hell, he'd been arrogantly sure that he could persuade her to stay.

Her absence was a significant shock.

He'd planned to convince her that her scruples were insignificant, to pull her into his arms and make love again…and again in the shower…as they had for those two passionate weeks in New York.

Not to awaken to this void of emptiness.

Nothing was going the way he'd planned. In the past two months his life had been turned upside down. What with Avery's betrayal, Jeff's weakness in the face of temptation, his father's death, the discovery that he had a half sister he'd never known…his world had gone crazy.

For the first time in his life, he didn't have the answers. He'd expected to hate Erica, to be able to forgive Jeff, to cope easily with his father's loss—after all it had been years since they'd spent time together. Most of all he'd been certain of his ability to persuade Avery to resuscitate their smoldering affair, until he grew bored.

But Avery had changed….

And so had everything else around him.

Eight

Avery stood behind the presenter's podium in the grand marquee waiting with some trepidation for Guy to join her. She took a sip of water and pretended to scan the notes she'd typed up on her laptop in the hours before dawn, when she should've been fast asleep.

It was not the prospect of facing a crowd that was responsible for her trepidation, only the thought of seeing one man. *Guy*. She'd sneaked out like a thief in the night. And paid the price by her inability to doze.

No doubt he'd slept like a baby.

When she caught sight of him coming her way, her heart did a somersault.

He was wearing dark trousers ironed to a knife-edge, and a white shirt that hung out giving him a rakish look. There was a faint line of stubble on his jaw that should have made him look untidy, but only made him more irresistible.

His gaze caught hers, and for a moment they both stilled,

then he gave her a faint smile. It widened, full of charm and promises. Empty promises…

Avery glanced away as he wound toward her side, checking around to see if anyone else had noticed that moment of jolting awareness between them.

No one sitting in the rows of seats appeared remotely interested.

She relaxed a little.

"You ran out on me."

The whisper as he placed a laptop on the podium beside her notes caused Avery to shudder.

"Hush!" She slanted him a frown. Then ruined it by adding, "You looked like a baby, all innocence and eyelashes."

A flush stained his cheekbones. "I can assure you, I didn't feel nearly as innocent as a baby when I woke up this morning…."

The loaded words caused a rush of heat. For a moment she half wished she'd given in to the reckless temptation to stay in his bed all night long. For sure she would've slept better in his arms than she had alone. She'd missed him from the moment she'd left.

Avery had a sinking feeling that she was about to cave to his demands. She reminded herself she simply wasn't the kind of woman who could sleep with a man without an emotional connection. And tried to convince herself that her hurt and anger at Guy had broken the emotional connection that had bound her to him.

She could never do pleasure for pleasure's sake.

Yet she knew she lied to herself. Because Guy still drew her like a moth to flame. God. How could she feel something so self-destructive about a man who felt nothing for her?

"…only to find that you'd gone."

His murmur was so low she barely heard it, but it was enough to make her stiffen her spine. He might not love her, and she might feel a lot more for him than she wanted, but she couldn't afford to forget that he only wanted her for sex—however much he wrapped it up in pretty words.

"Guy, stop it! This is my career, it's important to me."

She couldn't afford to compromise her career, her own professionalism for a relationship that was headed nowhere. She had to make him understand that.

"Yes," he said impatiently. "I accept that."

"Good."

But was this what she really wanted?

There would be no more nights of illicit passion. It would all be over. She would be well on her way to getting him out of her system—out of her life. She would never be the butt of a host of insinuations about a little gold digger sleeping with the boss.

It was all for the best.

She had to stick to her guns…and not cave in to his demands or her desires. Those would only cause her harm—even though the hold Guy had on her heart would make it all too easy to assent.

By contrast their second presentation five days later was all business.

Yet it belied the fact that Avery and Guy had fallen into a routine since the night she'd fallen asleep in his suite. Each day they would spend several hours going through recipes Guy wanted to add to the menus and seeking the perfect wine and beverage match. Avery also spent a couple of hours each day reviewing and training the restaurant and bar staff. In the evening, she and Guy would order in room service to Guy's suite and analyze the day's progress. There was a delicious domesticity about their relationship, and Avery stored up every memory.

After their speech, a trio of foodies came up to talk to Guy, and Louis, the French chef from Chagall's, told Avery that they'd done a great job. Then Trevor and Gavin were both there adding to the crowd.

Trevor took her hand and shook it. "Good job. You had me wanting to visit some of those California vineyards you mentioned."

"Thanks," she smiled at him when he dropped her hand. "Start with El Dorado, it's a winery I know very well—I grew up there."

Erica arrived with Christian, and the talk quickly turned to the December wedding they were planning.

"I thought we could serve champagne cocktails to the guests as they arrive. What do you think, Avery?" Erica asked.

"You could add a hint of cassis."

"Christian suggested I talk to you, Trevor, about where to hold the service since you live here."

"Hey, I'm a freewheeling bachelor. What do I know about weddings?"

Everyone laughed at the expression of mock horror on Trevor's face.

"But as president of marketing you're the perfect person to ask," Erica retorted. "Besides, apart from Christian, you're the only one who actually lives in Aspen."

Trevor spread his hands. "Of course I'll help. Hmm, your wedding will be in December, why don't you have Blake and Guy dress up as twin Santas?" Trevor suggested with a twinkle in his eye.

"I heard that," said Guy from the other side of the trio he was talking to.

Erica laughed. "They'd both need big white fluffy beards. I've gotten to know a few of the local vendors, I'm sure Dorothy from the yarn shop could organize something."

"Forget it," ordered Guy. And everyone laughed again.

"On a serious note, Christian and I will be using as many locals as we possibly can to help us prepare."

Guy had been watching Erica, but at this he broke in. "They'd like that. It's a good idea to include them—and it will have the bonus of garnering a lot of goodwill for Jarrod Ridge. Although I know that's not your primary motive for including the locals in the celebration."

Erica beamed at him, and Avery's heart turned to marshmallow. Any resentment that Guy might once have harbored toward his half sister had clearly been set to rest.

Discussion continued about the wedding for a few minutes more before Avery excused herself. As she walked away, she was aware of more than one pair of eyes on her retreating back.

"That woman is good-looking," Louis commented as Avery sauntered away.

Guy groaned, attracting Christian's sharp gaze. "You don't think so, Guy? Or is it just that you've been too busy to notice?"

Hell. "How could I not notice?" he retorted in response to his future brother-in-law's sly observation.

"Ah, so you have noticed." Christian's eyes crinkled with laughter. "What do you intend to do about it?"

Mentally Guy crossed his fingers. "Nothing."

"Then you're a fool," Trevor entered the discussion. "A sommelier and a restaurateur has to be a match made in the industry heaven."

"Now you're starting to sound like Dad. Who said I want to always be talking work to my lover?" Guy protested.

"At least you'd be doing something you love—think of me stuck here, torn away from everything I've achieved over the past decade." Gavin sounded utterly frustrated. "What was

Dad thinking setting his will up in such a fashion? I feel like I'm being buried alive."

"And think about how much you and Avery would have in common." Erica added her weight to the argument after a short pause.

Guy felt under siege. He could hardly disclose the one thing that would stop his family from matchmaking him with Avery. Once they knew that she'd cheated on him, they'd close ranks against her. But he'd never admit what a fool he'd been. "Just as well Blake has gone back to New York, otherwise you'd be canvassing him for an opinion, too."

"We can still ask Melissa," Erica grinned at him, an infectious smile that had Guy wanting to smile back.

"I haven't seen her all morning," Guy said as he thought about his sister. In fact he'd barely seen much of her all week, and when he had she'd been much more quiet than usual.

"She's probably run off her feet at the spa," Erica said, ever practical.

"She wasn't there when I went to the gym earlier," said Christian.

"She'll turn up." Guy raised an eyebrow. "Then you can start matchmaking her with some man—so start looking for someone suitable."

They all laughed, and to Guy's great relief talk turned away from Avery and back to Erica and Christian's Christmas wedding.

It was late afternoon before he caught up with Avery again.

"I wanted to talk to you more about the brief for the restaurants," Guy said to her as they walked up the pathway lined with a profusion of colorful flowers on the way back to Jarrod Manor.

"We can talk later."

He got the feeling she was about to disappear again. "Tonight. Come up when you're done."

"Let's meet in the sky lounge," she said quickly, "I'm still working on adding some more variety to the beer list for the Christmas season."

Didn't she know that anyone seeing him with her would be unable to miss the attraction she held for him? Even his family had noticed. "Maybe it would be a better idea to go check out some of the competition—we'll go to town, hit the bars and restaurants."

Avery's eyes lit up. "That sounds like fun."

Guy thought so too, and that way he wouldn't have to be so on his guard against his family's well-meant teasing. Nor would he have to disillusion them about what kind of person Avery really was. Although it was getting harder and harder for him to remember that himself...

She truly had bewitched him.

Avery decided she could easily fall in love with Aspen. Main Street was buzzing with activity. Pickups, Porsches and even a lovingly restored old Cadillac filled the lanes. And the stores—there was everything from Gucci to Macy's and burgers to up-market restaurants that the rich and famous were known to frequent.

Guy parked the SUV and Avery emerged from the passenger door to stare around like a wide-eyed child in a candy store. Couples strolled along the sidewalk, people spilled out of restaurants, families bundled together. Guy came round to her side. Avery scarcely noticed when he threaded his fingers through hers.

He pointed to a sign ahead. "There's the first bar where I thought we might conduct some covert espionage."

She wrinkled her nose at him. "Maybe I can get some business from them, too." It was a thought. That way, if things were going well between Guy and her perhaps she could stay longer than the month they'd agreed....

God! What was she contemplating?

"Not until you've completed your contract with Jarrod Ridge." He gave her a mock frown. "I'll have to get that signed and sealed as soon as we get back."

She gave a gurgle of laughter.

The next second she was spinning into his arms. His lips slanted across hers. Avery's laughter dried up. For a moment she responded, then she pulled away, and shook her hand free of his.

Oh, my, she was even holding hands with Guy.

To cover her confusion, she said, "Oh, an art gallery. Let's have a look." At that point even an abattoir would've elicited a squeal of delight. Anything to escape the confusion of being thoroughly and publicly kissed in the midst of Aspen's main street by Guy Jarrod.

"We're almost at the bar."

"I want to have a look." She needed a moment to regain her composure. "You can wait outside if you want. I won't be long." She dived through the door into the gallery, grateful for the respite. There was a row of touristy watercolor paintings of the town, and the gallery keeper was securing a round, red Sold sticker to one of them. Avery walked quickly past.

To the right was an alcove—it would've been a misnomer to call it a room. On the far white wall, plumb in the center, hung one canvas.

Avery stopped dead.

The power of that single painting sucked the breath out of her lungs with its sheer poignant beauty.

It was a while before she became aware of Guy standing silently beside her.

"Isn't this piece amazing?"

"Amazing."

There was a peculiar note in his voice. Avery glanced at him, a little resentful that he didn't share her enthusiastic admiration. His face was taut...pale.

"Guy?" Concern gripped her. "What's the matter?"

"I'll wait for you outside, okay?"

He shoved his hands into his pockets and turned away, his shoulders hunched as he headed for the door as though he couldn't get out fast enough.

What had evoked such a response? Was he annoyed because she'd pulled out of his too-public embrace? Or did his reaction have something to do with the gallery? She glanced back at the painting she'd been admiring when he'd come up beside her.

The painting was riveting. But disturbing enough to arouse such a strong reaction in Guy? Avery studied what should've been a peaceful subject. Perhaps. It was an abstract of a river. A swollen, moving river. There was turbulence in the dark, raging colors and the brush strokes. It was full of raw power... and anger. She couldn't take her eyes off it.

"It's compelling, isn't it?"

"Yes." Avery didn't glance up as the gallery keeper came up beside her. She was still trying to fathom what it was about the painting that aroused such strong emotions.

"Margaret Jarrod loved to paint the Roaring Fork—but this is one of her last works of the river."

Now Avery looked at him. "Margaret Jarrod?"

"Don Jarrod's wife." He pushed the round wire-rimmed glasses up his nose and glanced through the sheet window to where Guy was pacing the sidewalk. "I thought you knew it was her work."

Avery shook her head numbly.

"The whole town was very sad to hear about Don's passing."

"Yes, it was a tragedy for the family."

Questions swirled around her head. Guy had never mentioned his mother. She wanted to know everything. But it seemed…invasive…to ask the gallery owner while Guy cooled his heels outside.

"For everyone. The resort helped draw people to Aspen. The Food and Wine Gala that's on now is only one of the events that Don set up to benefit everyone in the town. There are fears that his children might abandon the resort—or, God help us all, sell it to outsiders."

Avery didn't know how to reply. "I'm here for the festival— and it's been wonderful" was what she settled for. With a smile she excused herself, "I must go, Guy is waiting."

Outside, Guy's face still wore that closed expression that had perturbed Avery.

With a burst of sudden longing she wanted the man who'd planted that joyful kiss on her lips back. But he'd vanished under the mask of stony indifference. Avery was determined to find him again.

She had a feeling it wasn't going to be easy.

But she'd always relished a challenge.

Best would be to put him off guard. To that end, she threaded her hand through the crook of his arm, "Lead the way. I'm ready to examine the competition."

The bar Guy took her to had attracted a well-heeled, casually-dressed crowd, where jeans were the order of the day. Mostly designer brands—Diesel, Calvin Klein. Although Avery also spotted the odd pair of working Levis—and footwear ranged from Jimmy Choos to dusty cowboy boots. But certainly these Colorado cowboys were ranch owners rather than hired hands, and the glitter at women's throats were diamonds rather than rhinestones.

The bartender took their order, and Avery turned her

attention to the cocktails chalked up on the blackboard behind the bar, then inspected the wine and beer list.

"Not bad," she said at last. She smiled her thanks when her drink arrived, while Guy paid for the round. Expenses, she told herself, suppressing the urge to object. This wasn't a date. He stuffed his wallet into the back pocket of his jeans and settled himself onto a wooden barstool.

"But you'd do better." He made it a statement.

"Of course." She set the wine list down on the counter and met Guy's gaze with confidence.

"Tell me how."

"I'd add some of the newer wines that are taking the country by storm." She warmed to her topic. "Then I'd look to add some international flair. What they've done here is to stick to the well-known Napa Valley wineries. They've done the same with the cocktails—the names might be risqué but there's nothing here that's new and refreshing. No imagination."

"What you're telling me is they've played it safe."

"Exactly!"

"You'd take more risks?"

The smile that tugged at his lips warned her of the trap she was headed for. "Forget it. I'm not going to go ballooning, Guy. I've got too much imagination."

The smile widened into a grin that had her innards melting.

"Did I even ask you to?"

"You didn't need to…I know where this is going." He was the most persistent devil she'd ever met. But she could be even more stubborn…and she would prove it.

Their next rendezvous was one of the most popular bar-and-grills in town, located in a brightly lit mall. They strolled along Mill Street, which gave Avery a chance to admire the store frontages. As they passed a busy eatery, Avery was startled by the loud sound of metal clanging.

"What's that?"

"Probably a bear."

"A bear?" She stopped and stared at Guy. "You're joking, right?"

He shook his head. "Nope. About a year back they started moving into town."

Just then two boys ran around the corner, one of them brandishing a Stop sign. Guy gave them a quelling look.

"Where did you get that?"

"Sorry, mister, we'll put it back."

With a scuffle they disappeared back around the corner, the sound of giggles following in their wake.

"Well, there goes your bear. Hope the little devils put it back."

"I'd say they were first-time offenders," Guy replied. "They didn't look sulky enough to be hardened miscreants."

"You recognize the difference?"

"I was a boy once upon a time."

"Well, at least it wasn't a bear this time," Avery said as Guy held a door open for her. "Boys I can handle—even in a place like Aspen which seems too glamorous for kids. But bears?" Halting at the bar, Avery wasn't ready to let the subject go.

The bartender had come over to greet Guy and take their order, and overheard her amazement. "You're hearing about our black bear problem?"

"So Guy wasn't having me on."

"Oh, no!" The bartender crossed his arms. "There was even a bear in the tree in front of the courthouse."

Avery blinked.

"In front of the courthouse?" Laughter bubbled up in her

throat. "Does that mean the sheriff had to arrest him for trespassing?"

Guy shook his head. "Nor the momma bear that stood watch while her cubs raided someone's kitchen after momma had broken the door down."

"Wow." Avery knew her eyes must be as wide as saucers.

"Don't feed any bears you might see."

"Don't worry, I won't." Avery loved Guy's honesty, his determination to protect the bears, and his insistence that people should take responsibility for their actions. "Trust me, I've got no intention of getting within a hundred yards of any bear."

"Ever the risk taker," said Guy.

And Avery gave him a sweet smile.

Sensing he'd missed out on a private joke, the bartender said, "Now what can I get you two to drink?"

"Make mine a strawberry margarita," said Avery. "I think I need it after all that bear talk."

"I'll have a beer." Guy made his selection and set the wine and beer list down.

Avery studied Guy, committing every feature, every nuance of his expression to memory. She watched as he brushed back the lock of hair that fell forward onto his face. "Have you ever seen a bear in the wild? That must be amazing—so long as it's a decent distance away."

"Plenty of times. And guess what?" Guy grinned across at her. "If you go up in a balloon you've got a good chance of seeing one too—and from a safe distance."

"Forget it!" She stuck her tongue out at him. "I'd rather be on the ground wishing I were in the air than in the air wishing I were on the ground."

He chuckled, his eyes warm and filled with humor.

"Let's study these menus, and see if the opposition is doing anything better than us."

Nine

Guy said no more about whatever it was that bothered him at the gallery during their outing. But an opportunity to learn more about him presented itself unexpectedly several days later.

"There's something I want to show you," said Guy interrupting the train of thought that Avery had been tapping into her computer while sitting at a table beside the sparkling resort pool.

She stretched lazily. She was feeling particularly content. A call from Matt had updated her on her uncle—he was almost back to normal. And earlier that morning her solo presentation had gone off without a hitch. "What is it?"

"You'll have to shut down your computer, because it will take a while."

Guy's gaze raked over her and Avery became conscious of how her blouse had pulled tight over her breasts. She lowered her arms.

"How much is a while?"

"My, but you're full of questions today."

The only way she was going to find out was to go with Guy. And her curiosity had been whetted. Busying herself with shutting the computer down, Avery packed it into its case, then rose to her feet. Guy led her through the spacious lobby scattered with tables and chairs and into an elevator.

"But this is the way to my room," she said as the doors opened to her floor. "What are you going to show me here?"

Avery followed him up a short flight of stairs, until he halted outside her room. "Open up."

She dug in her toes. "What's going on?"

"Get your swimsuit and a towel, we're going on a picnic."

"A picnic?"

He grinned, looking like he had no cares in the world. "Why not?"

"Haven't you got work to do?"

"It's Monday, the slowest day at the resort. The sun is shining, it's eighty degrees. The perfect day to show you the best swimming hole in Colorado. And test your theory that food tastes better outdoors."

"I suppose you've prepared the perfect picnic feast?"

"Uh…Louis did."

"In that case perhaps I should go on a picnic with Louis." Then she tensed at her stupidity and tried to think of an inane comment that would take the edge out her words.

But Guy didn't react with the suspicion she'd half expected. "No go. I organized the food, no one is hijacking my picnic."

Avery laughed and relaxed a little. If he was starting to trust her then they were making progress.

Better she accept that Guy was not going to cook for her.

Not because he hadn't had sufficient opportunity, but because for some reason he didn't want to.

She wished she could read him better, understand what drove him.

Today he was back to the easy charm that had attracted her that first day she met him. But she'd learned that the easygoing attitude also hid a reluctance to commit his heart. Avery didn't want the shallow charmer any longer; she wanted the complex, passionate man she'd glimpsed beneath.

Maybe a picnic would help unearth him.

Swiping her access card, she opened the room door. "Give me two minutes to drop off my laptop and change into a swimsuit."

Guy parked the black SUV under the trees and led Avery down an overgrown path to where the river flowed lazily into a calm pool in the lea of a large rock.

"Best kept secret in Colorado," he said.

"Gosh, the water is like a mirror." The willows along the river bank and the wide cobalt sky overhead were reflected in the flat surface.

"Not on the southern side of the rock, there's a waterfall there." With the picnic basket in one hand, Guy reached for her fingers with his free hand. "Come."

A bolt of pure happiness shot through Avery as his fingers threaded through hers. This was what she yearned for. This sense of companionship and contentment...with no hint of suspicion and distrust.

Near the edge of the river bank, in the green space under the largest willow, Guy set down the basket and let go of her hand. Then he tugged off his T-shirt and Avery caught her breath at the sight of his broad chest, his stomach tight with muscles that rippled in the sunlight.

Before he could see the effect his body had on her, she

turned away and stripped off her jeans and tank top to reveal the lime-green bikini she wore. By the time she reached the river bank, Guy was already moving across the ledge below the large, flat rock. He took three running steps and leapt into the water.

Avery edged down the bank until she stood knee deep in the swimming hole.

"Brr." She crossed her arms over her breasts to hide her puckering nipples. "It's cold."

"Of course it's cold. What did you expect? A hot tub?"

That brought back memories she didn't need revived right now, and a wash of heat replaced the water's chill. But when the water crept up her midriff, Avery forgot about hot tubs and nipples and squealed out loud.

"You should've jumped in while you had the chance."

Avery took one look at the wicked gleam in Guy's eyes as he swam toward her and sank hurriedly under the water.

"You beast." She came up stuttering at the shock of the river's chill. "You'll pay."

She splashed a wide arc of water at him.

He retaliated and within minutes they were engaged in a water fight, the cold forgotten, until they ended up under the stream of bubbles from the waterfall.

"That was wonderful." Finally worn out, Avery hauled herself out of the pool. Spreading her towel out on the grassy bank, she lay back in the sun, closing her eyes. Her stomach rumbled as hunger started to set in.

Peering through her eyelashes, she could see Guy sitting on his towel. Drops of water ran down his chest, causing her to follow their pathway over his chest, and belly…lower… to the waistband of his trunks. Those drops looked totally lickable.

She flushed, and jerked her gaze back to his face. "You always promised you'd cook for me one day."

"Did I?" His expression was impenetrable.

"Don't you remember?"

He shrugged. "I'm too busy to prepare food these days."

"You told me that back in New York." She braved his sarcasm. "You also said you missed it. That conjuring up dishes for your patrons didn't bring the same satisfaction as feeding friends and family."

Did he really not remember? Or was this another way of closing himself up to her?

"Sounds like I said entirely too much."

"Don't you recall the conversation?" Perhaps he had forgotten. Or never taken much notice to the promise he'd made. It only went to show how little their relationship had meant to him. It irked her that she was so forgettable he couldn't even remember their conversations.

Every word he'd spoken to her was engraved on her soul.

Don't call me again. Ever.

And she hadn't. If it hadn't been for Uncle Art falling sick, she'd very likely never have met Guy again. She'd sworn never to take an assignment in New York. Even among the millions of people the risk of encountering Guy was too great.

So maybe she was a 'fraidy cat.

Yet here she was trying to remind him he'd once promised to make her a meal. A fierce and stubborn determination crept in. "You said it the day that—"

"I vaguely remember."

Vaguely? That was even more insulting. Before she could object to his choice of words Guy had moved away to unpack the hamper.

"There's a selection of cheeses, a baguette, some pickles made at the resort, grapes and a nut terrine that is irresistible." Guy spread them out on a checked blue-and-white rug. Then he dug back into the hamper. "As well as a bottle of Pinot

Noir from the Sonoma Coast. No champagne today—I don't want to make you sneeze."

At least he'd remembered that! While it might not be exactly the same as having Guy prepare food for her, the spread looked heavenly. Avery's mouth started to water.

"I suppose I could settle for that."

Reaching forward, he tore off a piece of bread and scooped a little terrine on to it. "Try this." He offered it to her.

She took it daintily, closed her eyes, and chewed.

"Good."

Her eyes opened, and caught him watching her. "What are you staring at?"

"You're a pleasure to feed," he said simply.

"So feed me."

Guy's pulse leaped. But he took her at her word. Within minutes they'd demolished the contents of the basket.

"Just as well there wasn't more." Avery grinned at him and desire clawed at his gut in a way that was only too familiar. "A full stomach and warm sunshine would guarantee that I wouldn't move for a week."

He forgot about work. He forgot about the menu that Louis was waiting for him to finalize for the black-tie fundraiser for the coming Saturday night. His whole world consisted of Avery's sparkling blue eyes, and her wicked smiling mouth.

"There's still dessert," he murmured.

"Oh, I couldn't eat another thing."

"I think you'll find space for ripe black cherries." Guy shifted closer to her. The blue of her eyes deepened as she realized his intent.

"I love cherries."

They'd talked about cherries one evening at Baratin. She'd said she'd match the sweetness with a sauce of bitter chocolate. He'd argued that honey drizzled over would match better—he'd been teasing, his gleaming laughter-filled eyes had told her that much.

"There's a bottle of honey to complement it."

Her heart sank a little. No, he didn't remember. Or if he did, he didn't care enough to take her suggestions to heart. Avery felt unaccountably crushed.

"That will be nice," she said, subdued.

He took a glass bottle out the basket.

"But that's—" Her startled gaze shot to his.

"Chocolate. Bitter and dark." There was humor in his eyes. "I must have selected the wrong bottle." His brow wrinkled. "Silly me."

He hadn't forgotten!

That he'd remembered, taken the trouble to arrange something she'd said she liked was suddenly, overwhelmingly significant.

Avery helped herself to a cherry. "Definitely tastes better out here under blue skies. Sweet and juicy, all it needs is the chocolate."

His eyes darkened. "Very tasty."

"You haven't even tasted it yet."

"I don't even need the chocolate." He leaned forward and placed his lips against hers. His tongue swept across her lip. Slowly. Sensuously. Tasting the sweet juice of the cherry she'd eaten.

Her heart jolted, and began to race.

"Now I have," he whispered against her lips.

Avery pulled back. She had a feeling she was going to regret this later. For heaven's sake, he didn't even trust her. "Guy, where is this going?"

"All the way." His eyes were intense.

That wasn't what she'd meant. But she let it pass as he drew picked up the rug and drew her into the shadowy hollow under the willow. The rasp of his breath as she arched her back was enough for now, Avery told herself. When he was ready he would tell her why he shied away from intimacy.

It was up to her to convince him there was nothing to fear.

She put her arms around him and pulled him close. "Make love to me, Guy." *Love not sex.* Out here, feeling so close to Guy, she needed to make herself believe it was more than only sex. Even if she was deluding herself.

He didn't protest.

Instead he dropped his head and swirled his tongue through the valley between her breasts. Avery moaned. Her head tipped back, and the next moment she felt the stroke of his tongue against the arch of her throat.

She shuddered.

"Let's get this wet suit off." His voice was hoarse.

That gave her pause. "What if someone comes?"

"Oh, someone will come, all right," he growled.

Avery gave a shuddering laugh. "Don't joke."

"No joke." The eyes that burned into hers were scorching hot. "I promise."

For a moment her natural caution reared its head. Then passion took over. Under the canopy of the willow they were out of sight. Avery pushed all worries about interruptions, about tomorrow…next week, out of her head. Guy filled her vision, her world.

Lifting her hands she rested them on his shoulders. His skin was sleek and smooth under her touch, his muscles firm. She gloried in the warm hardness of him. He felt so vital, so alive.

"I'll hold you to that promise," she murmured as her hands traveled down and stopped at the barrier formed by the waistband of his board shorts. Languorously she tugged the laces undone. Slipping her hands inside the waistband she pushed them over his hips and down his legs.

By the time the wet bathing suit landed on the ground, he was hard and quivering. Avery sank down onto her knees, and heard him gasp as her mouth closed on him.

Seconds later he was tumbling her onto the rug, spreading her thighs. Touching her...stroking her with hands that shook. Until her body started to sing. Just when she feared she could take no more he slipped between her thighs and sank into her, filling her until she could think of nothing.

Except Guy.

Avery arched her back and gave a breathy moan of pleasure.

He lifted his head. "Okay?"

She nodded. "Oh, yes."

His lips curved. "I'm glad—for me, too."

She wanted to say that it could be even better. If he could only relax his guard, let her into his heart, and learn to trust her.

But she knew that if she voiced the intense thoughts his smile would vanish, he'd withdraw. Because the reality was that Guy didn't want a lasting relationship. Now was all that mattered to him. She was a fool to want more with a man who didn't even trust her.

So she bit her lip instead, closed her eyes, and focused on the connection they had.

Then he started to move and she forgot everything. Except the pure blinding silver pleasure of the moment.

Afterward they sat out on the sunny river bank and ate dessert.

The cherries and rich chocolate dipping sauce might as well have been stale bread and cold broth for all Guy cared. It tasted bland. Prosaic. It was Avery that he hungered for, her skin, her lips that he craved. Not food.

He couldn't take his eyes of her. She'd pulled a tank top on with the lime bikini bottoms. She looked so breathtakingly colorful, so alive. And she'd been so passionate, so giving… everything a man could ever desire.

Yet one part of him still hung back, knowing that she would never be what she promised.

There'd be other men. And in the end she would leave again. He had to steel himself. He couldn't afford not to keep a part of himself carefully in reserve.

"Guy—" she hesitated "—we need to talk."

"Let's enjoy the sunshine."

She fell silent. Then, "There's something I need to tell you."

No.

Whatever it was he didn't want to hear. "I don't need confessions." It came out more harshly than he'd intended.

He felt her grow stiff in his arms and he suppressed a sigh. Why couldn't she just be satisfied with what they had? With the joy of the moment? Why did women always have to complicate everything?

But he sensed this was important to her. That she needed to get whatever it was she wanted to talk about off her chest. Guy told himself he could take whatever it was. Hell, he'd already gotten over her fling with Jeff, hadn't he? He could get over whatever else she was about to reveal, too.

It wasn't as if he were emotionally invested in her.

They were lovers, not soul mates—he'd always scorned the very idea of those.

"Tell me," he said with a touch of weariness.

"Maybe now isn't a good time."

Typical. Guy stifled a burst of impatience. "Don't go all feminine on me. You can't start something then pull back."

"You're not making this easy."

He suppressed the urge to groan. They made fantastic love. All he wanted was to spend the afternoon lazing in the sunshine with Avery beside him. She had to go wreck the mood with her urge to make a confession he had no desire to hear. And she said he wasn't making it easy?

She drew a deep breath. "It's about that night with Jeff."

Heaven help him…this he most definitely did not want to hear about.

She must've read the reluctance on his face, because she said hurriedly, "That night, you need to know—"

"No. I don't need to know anything about that night," he interrupted. "It's over. Forgotten."

If he told himself that often enough he might start to believe it.

"It's not over," she said stubbornly. "It hangs between us all the time."

"Nothing hangs between us, as you put it."

Guy wanted to end this discussion. He hated the thought of her with Jeff, responding to his friend with the same glorious abandon she'd just responded to him with. He didn't even want to think about it, much less do a postmortem on the distasteful topic. Nothing would take away the pain of Jeff telling him what a wildcat she'd been in bed.

"Of course it does. I implied I'd slept with Jeff, when I hadn't."

He went still. She wanted him to believe she'd lied? "Why would you do such a thing?"

How the hell was he supposed to believe this when she'd just admitted to lying to him once already?

She glanced away. "Surely that's obvious?"

"Nothing is obvious." He rolled away from her and, propping his arms behind his head, gazed up through the bent branches of the willow to the fragmented pieces of bright blue sky beyond. He refused to feel relief…or hope. Jeff had told him she'd seduced him, and Avery had confirmed that. Now she was changing her story. The chances that Jeff had lied, too, were too remote to even consider. "Why don't you spell it out?"

"I was angry with you."

"With me?" Guy turned his head and stared at her incredulously. "What did I do?"

"You put your business ahead of me—just like you always do."

"Hold on a minute. Do you know how I worried about you? Waiting for you at Baratin—and you never arrived."

For a moment Avery caught a glimpse into the depths of hell. Her fury evaporated. That night in the spa he'd told her that he'd asked Jeff to arrange a cab for her and to let her know. Instead Jeff had decided to collect her himself. And she'd run. So why had Guy worried? "But Jeff told you I seduced him. Why should you worry about me?"

"He told me over two hours later. I came back to my apartment to see if by any chance you were there—even though you weren't answering your cell phone or the apartment phone—only to find a devastated Jeff."

"I left my cell phone behind on the sideboard in my hurry to escape."

"It wasn't in the apartment."

Avery searched for a logical explanation. "Then Jeff must've taken it."

"Every explanation you offer comes back to blaming Jeff."

Avery let the accusation go. "When did he tell you about the supposed seduction?"

"When I found him drunk as a skunk in my apartment. He was torn up with guilt for sleeping with my girlfriend."

"Who seduced him," she said with a snap of her teeth. Jeff had been very clever.

Guy's gaze bored into her. "He begged my forgiveness."

Another brilliant touch. "After he'd convinced you it wasn't the first time I'd tempted him." Oh, she could see how Jeff had played it. "He manipulated you."

He'd manipulated her, too. She'd never even paused to call Guy and check his story out. She'd been too outraged and hurt. So she'd simply cut her losses and run. Exactly as Jeff had probably intended.

Guy had deserved more.

Guy was shaking his head. "I don't think so. He was crying—it really cut him up. He blamed himself. He was even making statements that sounded dangerously suicidal."

More manipulation.

Yet how could she place all the blame on Guy for being taken in? She'd believed Jeff, too. Had it given her a convenient excuse to run? Deep in her heart she'd known that she and Guy would never last…he wasn't looking for a wife, a family. He'd told her, too often, how happy he was with his life just the way it was.

Taking in the shadows under his eyes, Avery decided he didn't look terribly happy now.

He looked strained…and tired.

She'd been so angry on the night of her birthday because he'd put work before her. She needed to try to get that frustration across to him.

"You told Jeff to get me a cab so I could meet you at Baratin." Even now it annoyed her that he hadn't bothered to leave his precious business and pick her up for their date. "At the time I thought you'd forgotten all about my birthday. Until Jeff arrived and told me you'd sent him to pick me up because you were too busy—"

"Wait a minute—"

Avery discovered she was shaking. "He made it clear he was supposed to be the appetizer for our dinner date—that he was the special surprise you'd promised me for a birthday I would never forget."

Guy straightened.

"What?"

The stormy expression on Guy's face only made her shake harder. He wanted her to bare her soul to him, while he watched her from behind slitted, shuttered eyes?

Sure thing.

Clearly he didn't believe her. She'd taken a risk telling him, and lost everything. In his eyes she was a gold digger, a slut, a liar. So what was she still doing here?

Avery stumbled unsteadily to her feet. "Take me back to the resort." His disbelief had withered the last bloom of hope. "I'll leave tomorrow."

It was all over.

She couldn't work with Guy anymore, couldn't bear to see him. There was too much love lost, too much hurt and heartbreak.

She'd find a way to explain to her uncle. At least the two presentations were over. She'd done Uncle Art proud....

"You can't—"

"I have to. I can't stay here." It was going to damage the professional reputation that she valued so highly to walk out in the middle of a contract. But she couldn't endure Guy's distrust any more.

Guy's hand closed around her elbow. "Avery, listen to me!"

She froze within his grasp.

The warmth of his fingers was at odds with the harshness of his tone. She glanced up.

"I'm listening."

"I never sent Jeff to have sex with you."

She started to laugh uncontrollably. She already knew that Jeff had lied to her. But there was a certain irony in saying, "I suppose you expect me to believe that? After all, Jeff told me, and you trust Jeff implicitly. Why shouldn't I?"

Guy's fingers tightened on her wrist and his skin stretched taut over his face.

"He lied."

"So you say. Did Jeff show you the bruises where I kicked him in the shin? He should've been limping, I can't believe you didn't notice."

"I didn't see him for a few days after he told me—" Guy paused "—that you'd begged him to make love to him. That it wasn't the first time."

"Now that is a lie." Avery lifted her chin. "You always believed Jeff. So it's pointless for me to deny it, isn't it?"

"What do you expect when you told me nothing about it at the time?"

"I called you—"

"After you'd already packed up and left."

"Because at the time I thought—" She broke off.

"Because you thought what?"

Because she'd believed Jeff.

She'd been put off balance by his turning up at Guy's apartment, knowing it was her birthday and that she was having dinner with Guy—information he could only have gotten from one person. Guy. Then there'd been the way he'd made himself at home accepting her offer of a drink, his presumption that she'd let him make love to her because Guy had gifted him to her.

A monstrous lie.

But she'd been too taken aback to question it. She hadn't trusted Guy....

"I thought that you were into sharing me with your friends—I didn't want that. Jeff was very convincing. He made it sound like it was the kind of stunt you two pulled all the time," she said, trying to justify it. "In the end I had to fight him off."

"Fight him off?" Darkness—doubt?—entered his eyes. "Jeff's not aggressive."

"You think I'm making this up?"

He ran a hand through his hair. "God, I don't know what to believe. I keep thinking you must've misunderstood Jeff—or overreacted to a joke he made."

"He'd been drinking. He wasn't joking. I had to kick him to let me go."

"You should've called me."

"I told you, I rushed out without my cell phone. I just wanted to get out," Avery confessed. "And frankly I was so mad at you. Right then you occupied the number one spot on my all-men-are-bastards list. Once I reached the airport I cooled down a little and rang you from a pay phone."

She'd needed him.

That's when he'd told her he'd leave her bags with the doorman and said, *It was fun while it lasted. Don't call me again. Ever.*

And cut the connection.

That had convinced her that he was angry with her for not fulfilling Jeff's drunken fantasies, and that Guy Jarrod was a total, hedonistic bastard. That she was well out of the relationship. To top it off, she'd had to catch a cab back to his apartment to retrieve her bags from a curious doorman. It had been the final straw in her humiliation.

Guy raked his hands through his hair. "Avery. I've been in business with Jeff for three years. I've never known him to hurt a fly."

"So you don't believe me," she said tonelessly.

It stung that he hadn't accepted her word. But she'd expected this. She could hardly whine about it. After all, her pride had caused her to make that ridiculous intimation that she'd slept with Jeff.

And she hadn't trusted Guy, either. She'd been so busy

thinking of herself as the victim, that she hadn't even realized she'd done Guy a disservice too.

They were both a pair of fools.

"I didn't say that I don't believe you. But I have to give him an opportunity to give me his side of the story." There was a hesitant note in his voice.

Was it possible that she was gaining ground?

"You didn't let me give my side when I called from the airport," she pointed out.

"Because I barely knew—"

"Because you barely knew me," she finished for him. "I was only the woman who'd spent two weeks in your bed." The woman who'd fallen in love with him. "What's that compared to male friendship?"

"Hey, wait a minute, this has nothing to do with sexism."

"Doesn't it? You think Jeff is less likely to lie to you?" Irrationally she ignored the fact that he had known Jeff for a lot longer than he'd known her. That there might be merit in his argument. But she wasn't in the mood to be reasonable right now. Her throat was tight with unshed tears. Damn Guy Jarrod. He was breaking her heart all over again.

"The point you're not getting is that Jeff didn't just walk out without a word and leave. *You* did."

The silence simmered after his outburst.

Guy clenched his fists and let out a hissing breath. "Look, I didn't intend to say that. I think we both need to calm down. I'll put the hamper in the SUV. Why don't you change out of that damp swimsuit?"

Ten

Avery ducked under the large willow tree and swapped her still-damp bikini bottoms for a panties and jeans, and started to untangle her hair and finger-comb it out.

Why had Guy been so wound up by the idea that she'd walked away from him? She'd never thought that would've caused any resentment at all. He'd made it more than clear that she wasn't an important fixture in his life.

Had she misunderstood his casual, carefree manner? Had she meant more to Guy than he revealed?

Avery put her bikini in her tote and hefted it onto her shoulder, then shook her towel out. But the actions were performed without thought. She couldn't get Guy's face out her mind.

Surely what she was imagining was insane? Guy had never cared for her—not in any way that mattered.

The snapping of a twig caused her head to turn.

"Guy?"

Instead of Guy she found herself looking into the furry black face and inquisitive eyes of a bear.

A very young bear.

A cub.

Oh, help! Where was Momma? Her towel falling from her numb fingers, Avery started to back up.

The bear started to sniff at the hedge on the far side of the willow. Leaves rustled on Avery's left. She whipped around in time to see a second large cub come gamboling into the green cave under the willow.

Damn.

Momma definitely wouldn't be far away.

Her pulse pounding, Avery eyed the trunk of the willow tree. It wouldn't be too difficult to pull herself up onto the lowest branch. Then she remembered the bartender in town saying that a bear had invaded the tree outside the courthouse.

Momma bear would probably have her butt before she reached the first branch.

The newcomer leapt on the smaller cub and they started to roll around on the thick mat of grass. Then the smaller cub rolled onto his feet and shambled over to her towel.

Get away, she willed.

He didn't heed her silent urgings. After sniffing it, he pawed it. The other cub joined in and before long they were playing tug-of-war with Avery's towel.

Where was Momma?

A loud snort answered that question. The bottom fell out of Avery's stomach as both cubs paused and pricked their ears, turning their heads toward where the sound had come from. Yes, that's right. Good babies. Go find Momma. Then they turned their attention back to the bright yellow towel.

Damn. Damn. Damn.

Avery knew she didn't have long before Momma came

looking for her recalcitrant cubs. But her legs didn't seem to want to work, a result of the adrenaline rush that the cubs' arrival had brought.

Dry-mouthed, she swallowed, but the coppery taste of fear stayed on her tongue.

She took another step back and came up against a wall of flesh.

"Easy," Guy whispered in her ear. "Keep still."

Her legs, already weak, turned to liquid with relief at the sound of his voice. Avery leaned back, grateful for his presence, the feel of his chest solid against her shoulders.

"Where's the mother?"

"At the river bank. I saw her when I came back."

Thank goodness he had.

"She'll come looking for her cubs."

Even as she spoke the cubs tired of the game of tugging and clawing at her towel. Dropping it, the larger cub trotted through the willow fronds and then after a few seconds the smaller cub followed.

"Whew." Avery darted forward to pick up her towel, then linked her trembling fingers through Guy's. "I have never been so glad to hear your voice."

"You kept your head. Although I will admit I got a shock when I saw the bear knowing you were nearby. When I heard the cubs cavorting I grew more worried. Luckily I found you before their mother did. Look," Guy parted the fronds of willow, "there's the sow."

Avery took in the black bear, her brown muzzle snuffling at her cubs.

"She can smell your scent on her cubs from the towel."

"Thanks—that reassures me."

Guy chuckled softly. "I'm not going to chase her away. Let's leave them to their world."

Avery was only too ready to follow him through the hedge

at the rear of the willow and scramble up the slope to where the SUV was parked. Once safely inside she said, "Strange as it may seem, I don't think I would've missed that experience for the world."

"What? You weren't terrified?"

"Oh, I was terrified all right. But it was worth it."

Guy shot her a narrow-eyed look. "You know what? I may still get you up in that balloon after all."

The first thing Guy did on his return to the resort was to close himself up in the wood-paneled study that had been his father's and put a call through to Jeff Morse.

Vivienne, his partner's very efficient PA, promised to have Jeff call him back shortly. An hour later, Jeff hadn't called. So Guy tried again. By the third call, Vivienne sounded uncharacteristically flustered as she advised that Jeff had just left to go hunting for a couple of days on a property that was out of cell phone range.

Guy set the phone down, propped his elbows on the walnut desk and stared for a long time at his steepled fingers.

Finally he moved to the computer in the corner of the study and booted it up. Fifteen minutes later he was satisfied with the e-mail he'd drafted. He hit Send.

Notifying Jeff of his intention to dissolve their Go Green partnership would provoke a response.

The picnic beside the river changed something between them.

Guy didn't raise the confession Avery had made about Jeff. But every night they met for dinner at Chagall's, obstensibly to discuss work, and afterward Guy would escort her to her room, and here they would make love. Not sex. Silent, desperate love.

After the first night Guy had refused to leave and they'd

ended up sleeping in each other's arms. Even though the next morning Avery had complained that he would be missed on the family floor.

"I have my own suite, it's self-contained," Guy said. "Melissa prefers the peace of Willow Lodge. Erica's moved out into Christian's house. Trevor's living in town. And Blake probably spends more time at airports commuting between Aspen and New York than he does at Jarrod Ridge. We're hardly living in each other's pockets. Too often I'm down in the kitchens checking the produce coming in from the markets early in the morning. Trust me, no one's going to miss me if I don't come to breakfast in the family kitchen."

When Guy put it like that, her reservations sounded absurd.

"You should move in with me."

"I don't want to be seen emerging from the private elevator early each morning," she said stubbornly clinging to her convictions. "People...staff...will talk."

"Then I'll fire them."

Her eyes went wide.

"Hey, that's a joke—bad one, but still a joke."

But it did remind her of the kind of power a man like Guy Jarrod had. He did have the power to make decisions about people's lives.

Even hers.

Later that day Avery felt restless and found herself needing more space than the resort, crowded with the continuous bustle of the Food and Wine Gala, allowed.

A drive into Aspen accomplished that. Without any conscious volition, Avery found herself back at the gallery where Margaret Jarrod's work hung. The gallery owner greeted her, and she smiled politely back before walking to the alcove in the back of the gallery to stare at the riverscape, as though that might give her the answers she sought.

Clearly Guy must've grieved when his mother had died. He'd missed her. Yet he never spoke about her.

Speak to me, Avery implored the painting. Help me understand.

But the picture remained a swirl of angry color and eventually Avery sighed and took herself off for a cup of coffee at a sidewalk cafe. Half an hour later she returned to her hatchback and made her way back to the resort.

On the stretch of tarmac just before the right turn onto the bridge that crossed the Roaring Fork River, a red sports car swerved to pass an oncoming white van.

Avery suppressed the fierce urge to scream. Faced by the sports car blocking her vision, Avery gritted her teeth and swung the steering wheel hard to one side.

The car bumped across the verge and lurched to a bone-jolting stop in a roadside ditch. Avery was flung forward as the airbags activated.

The radio hummed country music. Beyond the window she glimpsed bits of a tilted world. Dirt and shrubs and blue sky. Closing her eyes Avery said a silent prayer of thanks. When she opened them, it was to find herself staring through the windshield into a pair of feminine eyes.

"Are you okay?" The young woman asked, pushing her dark hair off her face.

"I think so."

Avery unclipped her seatbelt and tried to open the door. It was jammed solid. A wild sense of panic filled her. She had to get out!

"The car is on its side. You'll have to climb out. Are you sure you should be moving? Maybe it would be better to wait for the paramedics?"

"Yes, I'm fine." Avery couldn't bear the thought of being

trapped. The opposite door swung open. Avery clambered over the gearstick and hoisted herself out.

"I thought we were both finished when that idiot overtook me so recklessly." The other woman's expression turned to concern. "You're bleeding. There's a graze on your forehead."

Avery touched a hand to her head. "I'm fine—but I'm not sure if the other driver will be if I ever lay my hands on his throat."

"I've called 911, help is on its way."

Oh, thank God. "You must be an angel," Avery said with relief. "He was driving like a maniac, I didn't think I was going to be able to avoid a crash." Reaction was starting to set in.

"I thought we were all dead."

The brunette was ashen, too.

So she wasn't the only one who'd been terrified out of her wits for those moments, Avery realized. Moving off the verge, she flinched as she put her weight on her left leg. She felt unexpectedly shaky. "I'm going to sit down," she announced.

"Try putting your head between your knees."

Avery bent forward.

"Shock. My name is Nancy, by the way. Can I call someone for you? The tow trucks will probably be arriving soon."

"Guy."

"Which guy?"

Avery raised her head and caught Nancy's troubled look. The woman thought she was in shock. "Guy Jarrod—he lives at Jarrod Ridge."

"Okay." Nancy's face cleared, and she pulled a cell phone out the front pocket of her jeans.

Closing her eyes, Avery was dimly conscious of Nancy

telling someone what had happened. She concentrated on trying to stop the shaking that seemed to consume her.

At the sound of a vehicle slowing, she looked up.

"The paramedics are here," said Nancy, rising to her feet.

While the paramedics—a young beanpole of a man and a plump, motherly woman—tended to Avery, she tipped her head up to Nancy.

"How can I ever thank you enough for stopping to help me?"

The young woman shrugged. "It was nothing. It could as easily have been me who ended up in a ditch. And I didn't even get that idiot's license plate number."

"Me, neither."

They shared a smile.

The shaking had stopped. "Thank you for staying with me."

There was the sound of several vehicles pulling up. "Oh, and here's the tow truck, they'll probably take your car to town," said Nancy.

"I'll have to inform the rental company of the damage to the car." Avery winced at the thought. That was a call she was not looking forward to making. At least there would be insurance to cover the mess.

"Looks like your Guy is here too. So I'll be off."

Avery started. She was tempted to beg Nancy to stay.

"Is that sore?" The young paramedic asked, prodding gently around her knee.

"No."

"Avery!"

She jerked her head up at the sound of that all-too-familiar male voice.

"You are hurt!"

Guy moved faster than Avery had ever seen.

"Don't worry," she said, "it's only a graze—it barely stings."

"But that ankle will need X-rays," said the motherly paramedic. "We'll take you to the hospital."

"I'm fine."

"I'll take her." Guy was grasping her hand. It gave Avery an unexpected sense of comfort, of being cared for.

She let him help her to her feet but as she put her weight on her foot, her ankle crumpled.

"Ow."

"Definitely to the hospital." Guy's tone brooked no argument.

Yet Avery tried. "I don't need to go to the hospital. I'm sure it's nothing terrible—ice and elevation and it will be fine by tomorrow."

Guy shook his head.

"Guy, I'm fine. If you absolutely insist I can go to the medical center at the resort."

"You'll need X-rays."

"Don't be such a pessimist." Avery tried to make light of it.

But Guy only put his arm around her waist and said, "Lean on me. The sooner you get treatment, the better."

"He's right, my dear," added the motherly paramedic. "And if the only way to get you there is to let him take you, then so be it. But I need you to sign here for me." She produced a clipboard with a form.

With them all ganging up on her, Avery quit arguing and signed.

Once Guy had her in the SUV the drive to town went quickly. At the hospital a receptionist handed Avery a further sheaf of forms to complete. Full of questions about personal details. Medications. Consent.

Whether she was pregnant.

Pregnant. The word jumped out at her. If only...

She hesitated, before dismissing the sudden, startling fear. She wasn't pregnant. The test she'd taken—twice—had confirmed that. Before she could have second thoughts, she signed the form and gave it back to the receptionist with a smile.

"How long is the wait?" Guy loomed over the desk, his posture far from comforting.

"Not too long." The receptionist gave him a polite smile. "There's a coffee machine, feel free to help yourself."

Avery limped away to the seating area.

Guy came up behind her. "Can I get you a hot drink?"

"I'm fine."

Instead of settling beside her, Guy started to pace.

More out of a desire to give Guy something to do, than from thirst, Avery said, "I wouldn't mind a bottle of water, I saw a kiosk when we came in."

"Right."

Guy was gone before she could say more.

The receptionist caught Avery's eye and said, "Good idea to keep him busy."

Avery laughed in agreement. "I've only twisted my ankle, but he's behaving like it's broken."

The woman clucked. "Some men fuss when they're worried."

Avery didn't set her right. Guy wouldn't possibly be concerned about something so minor.

He still hadn't returned by the time Avery was ushered into an examining room. The doctor had kind brown eyes that looked years younger than her cropped, gray hair suggested.

"You've hurt your ankle."

Avery nodded and told her what had happened. "Just one

thing," she tacked on, "why do you need to know whether I'm pregnant?"

"So that we can take the necessary steps to protect the baby. It's always better to be safe than sorry. Is it possible that you may be pregnant?"

"I can't rule it out."

The doctor made a note on her pad. "We'll get that checked out to give some certainty in case we need X-rays. For now, let me take a look at that ankle."

Avery slipped her shoes off. "I took an over-the-counter pregnancy test—it was negative." The sinking regret that had swamped her returned for an instant. Reason told her that she wasn't pregnant. If she were, she'd be almost three months along by now. Surely she wouldn't have missed the signs?

It was impossible.

Yet since the first time Guy had raised the possibility of her pregnancy the thought had lingered, haunting her, refusing to dissipate, playing on her mind, recalling the dreams of motherhood…a family.

Wishful thinking?

No, it had been nothing more than dreams. Dreams that didn't—could never—include Guy.

Determinedly Avery shook herself free of the reverie.

"How does this feel?" The doctor's touch was cool on her ankle.

"No pain."

"What about now?"

Avery flinched. "That's tender."

There were more questions, and afterward the doctor said, "There is some swelling. It's probably only a twist, but I'd like to x-ray it just in case."

"It must've happened while I was trying to get out of the vehicle." Nancy had wanted her to wait for the paramedics, but she hadn't been able to bear the idea of being trapped inside the crippled car.

"The X-rays will confirm whether there are any fractures, but first let's get a specimen and check for pregnancy. I may have to examine you, too." The doctor lifted the handset of the phone on the wall. "Let me call the nurse to show you where the bathroom is."

Eleven

"You were right to be concerned," The doctor said ten minutes later as she leaned forward on her stool and studied Avery. "You are pregnant. When was your last period?"

Avery's ears started to ring and a numbness filled her. Frantically she calculated in her head. "I should've started my period this past weekend." But she hadn't. More desperately, she continued, "But the test—"

"When did you take the test?"

The test had failed. Despite the claims on the package of ninety-nine percent accuracy. How typical. Struggling with the daze of disbelief that had enveloped her, Avery tried to concentrate. "About two weeks ago."

"Too early to have shown." The doctor sounded very certain.

Avery stared at her in surprise. "What do you mean, too early?"

"By my estimation you're only about three weeks pregnant."

"Three weeks?"

That meant it had probably happened that night in the hot tub. Oh, God, how unlucky. And how lucky, too. She'd wanted a child…Guy's child…now it had happened, against all odds.

And against Guy's will.

Joy withered and dismay set in.

"I know it must be a lot to take in," the doctor said kindly. "There are always adjustments to be made." Glancing down at the form on her desk, she continued, "I see you work at Jarrod Ridge. I'll give you a card for a local prenatal group. Here's a diet sheet with suggestions of what might cause discomfort—don't forget to take plenty of folic acid." With a smile, the doctor added, "Congratulations. After you've had the X-rays done, come back and we'll talk about what to do to make that ankle as comfortable as possible. Ice and as much rest as possible for starters."

"Won't the X-rays harm the baby?"

The doctor shook her head. "You'll be protected by a lead apron. It will form a cone right down to your ankles. Baby will be perfectly safe."

Avery staggered back into the reception area, still reeling with shock.

Guy sprang forward.

"What did the doctor say?"

"Uh—" she gazed into his alarmed eyes. *I'm pregnant.* Yeah, that would allay his fears. Instead she forced a smile. "A twisted ankle. Nothing major."

Nothing major?

How on earth was she supposed to break the news? Guy had never wanted a long-term relationship. He considered her capable of sleeping with his friend, his business partner.

Of flirting with every eligible male who came her way. If he thought she was capable of that kind of treachery, surely he would never believe this baby was his? Particularly when she wasn't even sure whether he believed her about Jeff. Oh, God, Jeff was his friend, someone who was part of his everyday life. She'd prefer to see Jeff in hell. How could she bear to tell Guy that he was her baby's father when that would mean giving a creep like Jeff entry into her life? And her baby's life.

It was all enough to make her feel ill.

And that sensation had nothing to do with morning sickness—although that would probably not take long to follow.

Guy was staring at her expectantly. He must've asked her a question.

"I need to ice it and keep my weight off it, the doctor said," Avery bubbled, hoping that her response wasn't too far off what he asked.

His brow creased in a frown. "The room you have has a flight of stairs in the corridor. You can't stay there. Now you'll have to move in with me."

"No!"

Panic set in.

She couldn't bear to stay with him given all the tension between them.

"Avery, I swear I'll protect you. Your business credibility will not be compromised. But you need to be realistic. If you're going to have your foot up to rest it, you should have someone around."

"I'll be fine."

His jaw firmed. "We'll see."

A nurse came forward. "Ms. Lancaster? Follow me."

Guy caught her fingers. "Where to next?"

Avery shook her fingers free. "I'll be back as soon as the X-rays are done."

A backward glance revealed Guy pacing in the reception area, the bottle of water she'd requested still clutched in his hand.

"About time you got here."

Gavin, the next oldest Jarrod after him and Blake, came loping across the tennis court swinging his racket. Guy had called his brother to let him know that Avery had met with an accident, and he would be late for the game that had become a weekly fixture since their father's funeral.

"How is Avery?" Gavin brushed his light brown hair back from a face tanned to a shade of gold by the August sun.

"She banged her ankle." Guy shrugged, reluctant to let on how anxious he'd been. He hated hospitals. And all the while that they'd been there he'd kept worrying that something was going to go wrong. It had started with that dratted confrontation with the bear by the river. Hell, he'd almost been expecting today's call.

He had to get a grip.

Because Avery wasn't going to die.

She'd hurt herself—it was far from fatal. He wasn't about to share his baseless fear with Gavin, even though Gavin—not Blake—had been closest to him growing up. His twin Blake had always been able to say exactly what his father wanted to hear, whereas anything that Guy had said or done had been subject to criticism. His father had dismissed his drawings as useless. And when he'd told his father he wanted to be a photographer when he grew up, his father had bellowed so much that Guy had terminated his membership with the school camera club.

"She'll need to rest," Gavin said.

"I know." Guy unzipped his bag and pulled out his tennis

shoes. "But she's such a stubborn little thing, I doubt she'll listen."

Gavin gave him a swift look. "Sounds like you know her pretty well."

Oh, hell. That's right, Avery hadn't wanted his family—anyone—to know about them. He was so bad at keeping secrets. Especially from his family.

"Uh, we've talked a bit over the past weeks."

"A bit?" Gavin started to grin. "I heard about drinks in the sky lounge, dinners at Chagall's…you were even spotted out in town one night."

"All work—we were talking about the menus and beverages." It sounded so damn righteous. So he looked down and fastened his laces and added, "Truly."

The snort Gavin gave told him his brother hadn't bought it.

"I suggested that she stay in one of the family suites until her ankle gets better, but she refuses."

Gavin raised an eyebrow. "Your suite, I suppose?"

Avery would have his head if she overheard this conversation.

"The woman is injured." Guy tried to look affronted as he picked up his racket and zipped the cover off. "She will need help. Get your imagination out of the gutter, Gavin."

After giving him a penetrating stare, his brother said, "Perhaps she could stay with Erica and Christian."

Guy considered it. "Avery might feel like she's a third wheel—those two are nesting…planning their wedding."

"What about if she stayed with Melissa at Willow Lodge?" Gavin suggested.

"Willow Lodge is the cabin farthest from the Manor. It would be too hard for Avery to manage."

"Too hard for Avery to manage—or too far from your

suite?" Gavin taunted as they walked to opposite ends of the court.

Guy didn't answer. This was exactly the kind of talk Avery wanted to avoid. At Willow Lodge she'd have some space, some privacy. He concentrated on his serve. Fault.

After a double fault, he collected the balls and said, "You know, you might be onto something there. Willow Lodge would be perfect. Avery might be happy with that idea."

"You better take care," Gavin called a few minutes later when Guy served another double fault that gave Gavin the game. "You're distracted. Looks like woman trouble to me."

Ignoring the comment, Guy handed two tennis balls to his brother as they switched ends. "You still climbing the walls with nothing to do?"

Gavin said, "It's been extremely frustrating. A month ago I was in Namibia designing a wall for the biggest dam in that desert country. Now all projects are on hold. I'm twiddling my thumbs. Sitting around, waiting for Dad's estate to be wound up is driving me nuts." Opening his gear bag he pulled two bottles of water from the depths and handed one to Guy.

Pausing to open the pop-up top, Guy considered his brother's problem. "The Food and Wine Gala might not be the kind of thing that spins your wheels, but there must be some challenge you can sink your teeth into."

"I'll have to find something. Otherwise I might explore that old mine we played in as children. Maybe I can strike gold."

Guy laughed then tipped his head back and took a long swallow from the water bottle. Way back in 1879 Aspen had been the destination for a silver rush. Among the miners had been Eli Jarrod, their great-great-great-grandfather.

"Come on!"

With a start Guy realized that his brother was waiting to

serve. After tossing the bottle into his unzipped gear bag, he jogged back onto the court. "Ready."

The next few minutes passed in a flurry of action, during which Guy conceded most of the points to his brother. He sneaked a look at his watch. What would Avery be doing now? She'd gone to Tranquility Spa for a massage after their return. Surely that would be over by now?

A ball whizzed past him.

"Great ace," he yelled, hoping flattery would distract his brother from his moment of inattention.

"Ace? My eye." Gavin was laughing as he crossed to the other side and lined up for the final serve of the match.

This time the delivery was indeed an ace. No doubt about it. Guy shook Gavin's hand over the net and took the ribbing about where his thoughts had been for the duration of the game.

"You must be in love, brother."

Guy chuckled loudly. "Me? Not going to happen. I was thinking about what to do to keep you busy. Can't have you going insane with boredom."

He shifted under the unerring focus of Gavin's gaze.

"I always thought that when you fell for a woman you would fall hard," Gavin said finally. "Looks like it has happened at last."

"Don't kid yourself," Guy growled.

"Who's kidding whom?"

Guy had a sinking feeling that despite his wide-eyed mock innocence Gavin might be right, that he was indeed teetering on the edge of the precipice yawning ahead of him.

The vision was not comforting.

* * *

Guy paused for a moment at the door of the premier spa room that Melissa had told him Avery was using.

Avery was sitting on a ledge in a long pool. Water lapped at the top of her bikini-clad breasts in little waves. It rushed over an angled sheet of granite into the pool, sluicing over Avery below. Guy knew from experience that the water was hot—but not as hot as the next waterfall along.

Below the lime green triangles of her bikini top, her hands were touching her tummy with long, slow strokes that he found incredibly arousing. She wore a dreamy expression he'd never seen before.

"What are you thinking about?"

At the sound of his voice Avery started. Her gaze shot to his…then away.

"Guy."

She didn't sound delighted by his presence.

A feeling of déjà vu crept over him as he stepped into the room and closed the door.

Avery gave him an uncertain smile.

"How are you feeling?" he asked coming closer.

Her face cleared a little, and she laced her fingers together. "A lot better, thank you. Joanie has magic hands and Melissa made sure she pampered me to death."

His face softened at the mention of his sister. "Melissa has always been the nurturer in the family. I've just organized for you to stay with her for the night."

"But I can't just descend on her!"

"Of course you can—she's looking forward to the company."

"I'll consider it." Avery sank deeper into the water and her nose tilted up into the air.

He started to grin. Was it possible that his little spitfire was mad at him for doing something for her own good? "It's already sorted out."

She glowered at him.

She was cute when she was mad, and he had a feeling she was going to be madder still. Guy pulled his shirt over his head in one, swift movement, revealing a broad, muscled chest.

"What are you doing?" Avery shrieked.

"Easing out my tired muscles." In two paces he'd reached the door, and locked it. Next he toed off his sneakers. When he shucked off his tennis shorts, Avery closed her eyes.

He slid in behind her and pulled her up against his naked body.

"Guy!"

He kissed her nape. The skin was warm and steamy, and her hair was swept up on top of her head. Irresistible. "What?"

"You shouldn't be in here!"

They'd done this—and more—before. Already his body was hardening at the memory. But this time he had no intention of making love to her. Although Avery didn't know that. This time he just wanted to hold her.

"Give me one reason why not?"

"We work together—I don't want anyone to know we're involved."

"I'm not going to make love to you. I came to see if you're all right." He put on his most innocent expression, but it made no difference—she couldn't see it at this angle.

"I'm fine. And I sure thought you were making love to me. Because you're kissing the wrong part of me better."

His husky laugh caused the soft bits of hair at her neck to dance. "I'll kiss whatever part you want me to." He blew lightly onto her neck and felt her quiver. So responsive.

He tightened his arms convulsively around her.

"Thank goodness you're safe."

The images that had flashed through his mind when a young woman had called to say that Avery had been involved in a car accident...

Guy shivered. He never wanted to re-live those excruciating moments.

The thirty seconds it had taken to get confirmation that Avery was alive were amongst the longest of his life. The piercing pain had been a thousand times worse than the two hours he'd spent waiting for her at Baratin the night of her birthday. Because now he knew what it felt like to lose her...

He'd spent forty-nine days without her.

After the past three weeks he was starting to feel like he never wanted to let her go.

Avery tilted her head back. "I'm a lot tougher than I look."

"My mother thought she was, too." The words came from nowhere. He hadn't even thought about Mom for days. He usually tried not to talk about her at all. The topic always led to grim silences. But suddenly he couldn't prevent himself saying, "She promised me and Blake that she would beat the cancer."

Turning over, Avery looked up at him, her eyes luminous. "I'm sure she wanted to more than anything in the world. A woman with five young children would not want to leave them."

"I was foolish enough to believe her, in the way a six-year-old does. I thought she'd get better." How could he explain the devastation that he'd felt returning from a night at a friend's home to discover that his mother had been taken into the hospital, that she'd passed away? "She refused to have chemotherapy, you know. She chose to die, to leave us all. How can a six-year-old ever be expected to understand that?"

Avery slid up and pressed a kiss against his lips. "You poor little boy."

Hell. He didn't feel very much like a little boy right now. Not with her lying breast to hip along his body, her legs tangling with his. He gave a groan. "Avery, I got in here to hold you, to comfort you, not to make love. But you're making it very hard."

A wicked sparkle lit her eyes and she moved her body against his. "Am I?"

The little witch.

Guy groaned again. "Have mercy…and don't move."

"Why not?"

He swallowed. "You might jolt your ankle."

"My ankle is already feeling a lot better."

But she shifted and slid onto the seat beside him. Guy wished she'd stayed where she was. Yet if she had, the temptation would've been too great to resist. Instead he placed an arm around her shoulders, marveling at the tenderness that welled up inside him, the contentment that merely holding her brought. It wasn't something he'd experienced before.

Placing his index finger under her chin he raised it, and sealed her mouth with his kiss. Guy let himself sink into her… into the soft femininity that was Avery. Sweet. Feminine. Unique.

His.

When the kiss was over, he stared down into her blue eyes, stunned by how she'd inveigled her way into every crevice of his life in such a short space of time.

She blinked, and the spell was broken.

"There's something I have to tell you." She sounded subdued.

Guy wanted to shout "No." He didn't want to hear anything

that might break this accord that lay like a golden thread between them, joining them in a way that was somehow special.

Yet he found himself saying, "What is it?" while he hoped furiously that there were no further revelations about Jeff, or anyone else in her life, to follow.

The deep breath that she took warned him that he wasn't going to like it. But what she did murmur knocked the guts out of him.

"What did you say?"

She shifted in his arms, and Guy realized he was gripping her uncomfortably. He instantly slackened his hold.

"I'm pregnant," she repeated more loudly, edging away from him.

"How?" His head spinning, he asked, "Forget that. Have you known all this time?"

She blinked. "What do you mean 'all this time'?"

"Since being at Jarrod Ridge."

"Are you asking if this is the reason I came to Jarrod Ridge?"

He hadn't quite thought that far ahead. Now he considered it. Was this why she'd come? Guy shifted in the hot water. Had it been nothing to do with her Uncle Art at all?

Maybe it was what his subconscious mind was asking.

"Yes." His tone was terser than he intended as he tried to process the information that Avery was going to have his baby.

She slowly shook her head, and he could've sworn that the divide between them grew—even though she didn't move. "I only discovered today at the hospital."

"You've had symptoms?" And she hadn't bothered to reveal anything to him by word or action? He felt unaccountably put out.

"Nothing obvious. In fact, you started me worrying when

you asked whether there'd been any repercussions after our time in New York. I hadn't even thought about it. I bought a test from the drugstore—"

"So you had a suspicion that you were pregnant." Guy found himself glaring through the water to the pale skin of her stomach just visible through the swirling water. He couldn't see any sign that made her look remotely pregnant. "Thanks for letting me in on the secret."

"Hey, hear me out." She turned her head so that he looked square into her face. Her skin was dewy from the steam, and her eyes had darkened. She'd never looked more beautiful. "The test was negative—I took it twice. I wasn't pregnant then—"

"But you're pregnant now? How does that work?" Guy's brows shot up. "That *is* what you're trying to tell me?"

"Yes!" She was breathing quickly, her breasts rising and falling. "That's exactly what I'm saying. And before you even think of accusing me of trying to fob off someone else's baby on you—"

"That never occurred to me," Guy said heatedly, forgetting all about her breasts at the accusation. "Whatever gave you the idea I'd think that?"

"Your reaction to seeing me with Matt?"

Well, she had him there. He couldn't precisely argue without revealing his gut-grinding jealousy before he'd discovered Matt was her cousin.

"Your idiocy over Todd." She raised an eyebrow. "Warning me away from Louis? Need I go on?"

Guy started to feel very foolish. "Are you sure you're pregnant? It could be a mistake."

"Stop clutching at straws, Guy. I'm probably pregnant."

"Probably pregnant?"

But she didn't laugh as he'd intended at his emphasis on the absurd way she'd put it.

"I *am* pregnant, Guy. I know it's the last thing you want in your life. So I have no expectations of you. You are free. But you need to know I'm going to keep this baby."

He stared at her. What did she expect him to say to that?

Of course he didn't want a child—he didn't even want a wife, or a partner, or a significant other. He was quite happy the way his life was.

But he wasn't ready to lose Avery from his life either. For days he'd been dreading the idea of her leaving. He was no longer free—nor did he wish to be.

It struck him that the baby would give him a great reason to keep her in his life, without having to define to himself—or to her—exactly what their relationship was.

"Avery—" under the water he placed a hand on her thigh "—this gives even more reason why you should move in with me. You're pregnant with my child. That's hardly the kind of thing you can hide for very long. It's bound to come out."

Her thigh tensed. "You mean we should set up home together?"

Home? He wriggled like a trout hooked by a particularly attractive lure. "I was thinking we should live together and see how things work out."

She put her hands over her face. "Guy, a baby is about as lasting an arrangement as anything can be. It brings responsibilities like motherhood…and fatherhood. You don't have to assume that responsibility if you don't want to. I absolve you."

She was deliberately misunderstanding him.

Guy gave a sigh to vent his frustration and increased the pressure of his hand to make sure she didn't try to bolt. "Dammit—" he hesitated "—it's hard to take in. I never wanted a family."

"That's why I told you I'm not expecting anything of you."

Her hand closed over his. "Please understand I'm not trying to trap you."

"I know that." His certainty surprised him. His outburst had been boorish—the situation they were in was as much his fault as hers. He'd acted recklessly that night in the hot tub, and they'd both reaped the consequences. "And it's no longer about what either of us want. I'm sure this is every bit as much a trap for you as for me. The last thing you must want is a baby—particularly as your work is going so well."

After the Food and Wine Gala was over Guy had no doubt she'd have more work offers than she could handle.

"Not at all. I've always wanted a family…and kids." That dreamy look was back on her face.

Guy's heart stood still.

Sliding his hand out from under hers, he wondered if this had been a trap he hadn't even suspected? Giving her a narrow stare, he said, "Did you deliberately not use protection?"

"No! I stopped taking the Pill when I went back to California. I'd sworn off men." She gave him a wry smile. "And contrary to popular belief, I didn't come to Jarrod Ridge expecting to have an affair."

Ouch.

Was this a trap? If it was, hadn't he deserved to be caught? He hadn't taken precautions that night in the spa, even though he'd taken great care every time since. But once was all it took…

Avery stood up in the water and said, "I'll be going back to California in four days. There's no point in my moving in with you and telling the world that your mistress is pregnant with your baby."

Before he could temper his reaction, Guy burst out, "That's insulting to us both. You wouldn't be my mistress."

"Scared you couldn't afford me?"

Beads of water streamed over her curves…curves that

Guy knew intimately. But Avery was so much more than a sexy body.

He tore his gaze away. "Don't demean yourself! You're far too proper, with too much sense of your self-worth, to ever have accepted such an inequitable relationship—and I have too much respect for you to suggest it." Avery was far too independent to be any man's mistress. Although Guy was sure there were men who would've loved to have decorated her with diamonds and paid for her upkeep. She was smart, sexy and spirited. What more could any man want?

She looked stunned by his heated defense of her. What could he say? It had startled him, too. He justified it by adding, "My dad would've torn a strip off any of his boys for making a decent woman such an offer. He always said that honor was part of the Jarrod name."

Avery took two towels off a shelf, arranged one at the edge of the pool and sat down.

"A bit of a double standard, hmm? He must've kept a mistress, otherwise there would be no Erica."

"He didn't keep a mistress—not while my mother was alive." Guy glared at her for even suggesting that. Then he conceded, "But he did seduce another man's wife. Not much honor in that, I have to agree." Which was only one of the reasons he'd so resented Erica's existence. It went to prove that his father's high standards were nothing more than hypocrisy.

"Maybe he was lonely," suggested Avery.

"Lonely?" He shook his head. "That's stupid. He had a family—maybe we were farflung, but we were his children. He had Jarrod Ridge...the business empire he always wanted." Had it not been enough? Was Avery right? Had his father been lonely? Guilt pierced him. He shoved it aside, and focused on the woman who had turned his world upside down.

Leaning forward, Avery started to pat herself dry with the

second towel. "I think it would be far better for me to stay with Melissa as you've arranged, and for no one to be any the wiser about my baby."

Her baby? What about his rights? The surge of primal possessiveness took him aback. If Avery was planning to deny him access to his own child she was in for a surprise.

But it wasn't worth fighting now. They both needed time to absorb that they were going to be parents.

Finally he sighed and pushed his damp hair out of his eyes. "If you'd rather stay with Melissa, I'll take you to Willow Lodge."

Twelve

Willow Lodge oozed mellow serenity.

It was set away from the main resort complex, in a spot sheltered from the winds. Inside, the walls and floors were crafted from wood the color of honey and dramatic picture windows looked out over the willows for which the lodge was named. The fragrance of lavender and beeswax lingered in the air, and Avery found herself instantly unwinding.

And Melissa did everything to make her feel comfortable.

"Treat Willow Lodge like your home," Guy's sister said.

Avery took Melissa at her word. After sleeping under a down comforter and having a leisurely breakfast, Avery propped her leg up on a footrest in front of a window overlooking the willows and showing glimpses of the river beyond.

A constant trickle of visitors kept her entertained. Guy

was the first to arrive. Shortly after Melissa departed for Tranquility Spa, he came through the back door.

"How's the ankle?"

"Much better." Avery turned her head. Guy wore dark trousers and a black-on-white striped long-sleeved shirt with elegant European panache. The years he'd spent in France showed. She forced herself to stop gawking at the man like a lovelorn teenager.

He came closer and his breath was warm on the top of her leg as he leaned down. "No sign of swelling."

"Only a little bruising." With her fingertips Avery found the tender spot.

"It will go all the colors of the rainbow before it fades."

Avery groaned. "I hope not." He was so close that she could detect the subtle green notes of moss and musk in his aftershave. "I'm keeping it iced. It's helping—even though it's freezing."

"Good."

Avery wrinkled her nose at him. "You wouldn't be saying that if you were the one wearing an ice pack."

He hunkered down beside her, and put his hand on her ankle. "Probably not."

A delicious warmth cruised through her at his touch. Avery had thought her ankle too numbed by cold to respond to stimulus.

Not so.

When he started to move his fingers in little circular strokes her breath hooked in the back of her throat. His hand stroked up her calf, across the back of her knees, and tantalizing shivers followed. The taunting fingers stopped just below the hemline of her fitted dress, and she knew if she tried to protest her voice would be nothing more than a thin thread of sound. Then Guy would know precisely how much he was rattling her composure.

She glanced away, only to be transfixed by the sight of his long, square-tipped fingers caressing her flesh.

She inhaled a deep, steadying breath, and his heady male scent filled her senses.

How could one man have such an impact on her?

Only him.

Ever.

She feared it would only be Guy for her, all her life. And now she was pregnant with the baby he didn't want. It was over. He'd made it crystal clear he didn't want a wife… children…a family.

On Monday she was returning to El Dorado, to her family. Undoubtedly Guy would be amiable, offer support; Christian would be asked to negotiate the terms of any agreement, which she would insist on being kept confidential. Perhaps Guy would even offer to do his duty and see the child on the odd occasion. But Avery fostered no illusions that Guy would want to be actively involved with his child…or with her. She'd likely have more contact with Christian than with Guy.

At least she would have his baby….

She glanced up into his eyes. And stilled. There was an emotion she'd never seen exposed. A mix of tenderness and desire. Or something else?

Slowly he removed his hand from her leg. "I better get going. Otherwise I might not get to work today—and with the charity auction fundraiser tomorrow night, there's a lot to do."

Avery's heart skipped a beat.

For what seemed like a lifetime their eyes held. Then he leaned forward and kissed her. It wasn't like any of the kisses they'd shared before. It was gentle, tender, with the promise of passion in the way his lips moved on hers. And it left her yearning for more.

Then he pulled away and rose to his feet. "I'll be back later. Take care of yourself."

It was only as he walked away that Avery realized that despite his concern for her, he'd never once mentioned their baby....

After Guy had left, Erica dropped off a pile of magazines, and Avery discovered that they both shared a passion for collecting recipes and baking.

"Christian has a meeting in town tonight, so I'll come by with some ingredients to bake an apple pie," Erica promised.

Avery agreed in a rush. Guy had said he would return. The more people around to act as a buffer, the better. Guy clearly had no intention of talking about the baby, and nor did she. It would only cause tension and misery between them.

Erica had only just departed when Gavin and Trevor trooped in to see how Avery was getting along.

She was rather touched by the concern the Jarrods were showing her.

Late that afternoon Guy returned with food he'd had Louis rustle up in the kitchens at Chagall's. So by the time Melissa came home from the spa, the table was laid and candles lit, giving the honey tones of the lodge a cozy warmth.

"I seem to have taken over your home," Avery told Melissa apologetically.

"I don't mind." Melissa smiled at her. "It's nice to have company."

"But you've always said you wanted peace," Guy protested. "If you're lonely, you should come and stay in one of the family suites at Manor Lodge. In fact, there are two spare ones right now."

"I'm not lonely—and having Avery as company is different from living with you guys." Rolling her eyes, Melissa said to

Avery, "Believe me, sometimes a girl needs a break from her brothers. It was a pleasant surprise to discover I had a sister when Christian revealed Erica to us."

Avery slid her gaze to Guy to see how he was reacting to Melissa's revelation. But she detected none of the resentment she'd half expected.

"So that's a roundabout way of saying you're welcome to stay for as long as you like," Melissa smiled at Avery, "but my brothers are not."

Guy howled in protest.

Avery started to giggle. "Hey, I know exactly what Melissa means."

More laughter bubbled up in her throat as Guy glared at her.

"Traitor!"

"I was two when my parents died. I was lucky enough to be taken in by my aunt and uncle and I grew up with my cousins—four boys. Believe me, I always wanted a sister, too."

"Hey, now you're both ganging up on me."

"Wait until Erica arrives, you'll be outnumbered three to one," said Melissa with sisterly satisfaction.

Guy gave her an evil grin. "I'll have to call in reinforcements."

"No!" Avery and Melissa chorused. They glanced at each other and started to laugh.

When Erica walked in, she paused in the doorway. "Sounds like a festive dinner."

"Avery mentioned you were coming to bake a pie. There's more than enough food, so join us for dinner."

"That sounds like a great idea."

But Avery wondered if she was the only one to detect Erica's hesitation. Her hand touched her tummy. These people were her baby's family…she would've loved her baby to have grown up among them.

If only things could've been different. Not going to happen. Even though she'd needed Erica and Melissa present to stop the awkwardness between her and Guy, she was a little irritated that he'd made no attempt to corner her and discuss the baby.

It only underlined the fact that this was no romantic daydream; this was real life and sometimes it didn't work out quite as planned.

Guy had hoped for time alone with Avery.

The shock and terror that had followed her announcement that they were expecting a baby had started to wear off. Perhaps it was for the best that their talk didn't happen tonight. Avery deserved time to recover from the accident, and he could do with more time to get his head around the idea of the baby so that he could decide how he was going to handle the problem.

After they'd finished dinner, Guy found himself slouching on a barstool in the kitchen watching as the three women worked around the preparation island in perfect harmony. His sister, the half sister whom he'd treated with extreme wariness until very recently…and Avery.

Guy couldn't quite decide how best to describe his relationship with Avery.

He frowned as he watched her kneading the dough for the apple pie, her small hands moving with sensuous grace. Melissa had cut the apples into elegant slices and at Avery's insistence she settled down on the kitchen stool beside Guy and started to rub the small of her back.

"Did you hurt your back at work?" he asked.

"I'm not sure what I've done. It's aching a little."

For a split second the image of his mother rubbing her back in a similar fashion flashed through his mind.

"What is it?"

"Nothing." Then Guy shook his head to clear the image, and said more truthfully. "Actually, for a moment you reminded me of Mom doing that. I think she used to rub her back as well."

"How old were you when your mom died?" asked Erica from the other side of the kitchen island.

"Six."

Guy hadn't been there when she'd died. He'd been sleeping over at a friend's home. For years he'd been convinced if he'd been home she might not have died. It was his fault.

Blake had gotten to say goodbye. So had Gavin and Trevor and his father. Even Melissa, though she was only two at the time.

Guy had pretended he was fine, and retreated behind a happy-go-lucky facade that everyone except him accepted as the real Guy. He'd resolved never to give another human that much power over his life.

The only sound that broke the silence was the slap of the rolling pin on dough as Avery rolled it out.

Erica was sprinkling cinnamon over the apple slices. "I've heard plenty about your dad but not that much about your mom." Giving him and Melissa a swift glance, she added, "I don't mean to be nosy, but I've wondered, and you are my family now."

Melissa gave a sigh. "Dad changed after Mom died. He was very upset by her death, so we avoided talking about Mom at all."

"How sad!" Avery stopped rolling. "I never realized how lucky I was. My uncle told me all about what my mom had been like growing up. And both my aunt and uncle regularly pulled out the photo album and showed me photos of my parents' wedding, of my first birthday party. I always knew who they were."

"Guy used to stare at Mom's paintings."

Melissa clambered off the seat and started to cut the left over pastry into strips, while Avery pressed the dough into a baking tin. Erica carefully arranged the apple slices on top of the dough.

"He used to say they made him remember Mom, what colors she liked and how she smelled," Melissa continued after putting the pie in the pre-heated oven, "but Dad sold all the pictures—he didn't want anything to remind him of Mom. We've since managed to buy some back."

"Dad also got rid of the camera he and Mom had given me for my sixth birthday."

Melissa looked horrified. "I never knew that."

He didn't look at Erica...or Avery. "I used to say I wanted to take photos like Mom's paintings when I grew up. I suppose it was too painful for him to contemplate. Later I bought my own camera and joined the school's camera club."

"I remember that," said Melissa. "You wanted to be a photographer."

"But Dad wanted me to do a business degree. Like Blake." Guy shrugged. "Eventually we compromised. I did the business degree, but only after he agreed to let me go to culinary school."

"How could he do that?" Erica protested.

"Easily. He was Don Jarrod, he was used to imposing his will on everyone around him."

All three women had fallen silent, their eyes focused on him with varying degrees of...pity.

Guy forced an easy smile. "It was a long time ago. At least I got to do something that I loved. Something creative and satisfying, yet still lucrative."

"But you never forgot your mom," said Erica.

"No, I didn't, but it took a long time for me to stop resenting her for leaving us," he admitted in a rush of honesty. "Losing her wrecked Dad's life. I didn't like the kind of man Dad became after Mom died."

"How did he change?" Avery asked in a tentative voice. She'd propped her elbows on the island and her chin on her hands.

Guy shrugged. "None of us could do anything right."

"He had huge expectations of us all and wanted us to stay in the business doing what we were told," added Melissa, shaking out her blond hair. "Just like Guy said."

"And he let you go to France?" Avery's voice was filled with disbelief.

"He tried to stop me. He'd planned for me to stay closer. I won that battle." Even all these years later Guy could remember the satisfaction he'd gained in that moment.

"Guy wasn't the only one who left. Blake went to New York and I escaped to Los Angeles where I ran an ultra fashionable spa," Melissa added from where she'd perched herself back on the stool beside him. "And once Gavin finished university, he worked all over the globe, as far from home as possible. Only Trevor stayed in Aspen—yet even he wouldn't work for Dad at Jarrod Ridge."

"So Don Jarrod's empire was in danger of crumbling." Erica said, her hands busy as she wiped the surface of the island clean. "But he had the last say from beyond the grave, and forced you all to come back and work together if you wanted anything of the estate—"

"Don't forget his will also introduced you into the family," interjected Melissa. "You also stand to inherit a share of his empire."

Erica put the cloth in the sink and pulled a face. "Much to everyone's dismay."

"Not mine," said Melissa quickly. "I told you I always wanted a sister. You're part of the family now."

There was a silence.

Avery was looking at Guy expectantly. What did she expect him to say? That he wanted another sister? That he was glad to discover Erica's existence?

Hell, no. It only proved that his father had not been as inconsolable as Guy had foolishly believed all his life. So much for his resolve never to love a woman as faithfully as his father had loved his mother because he didn't want to risk the same heartbreak. He'd never been the kind of man who dug too deep into feelings, and he wasn't about to start now. It hurt too dammed much, revealed too much of what was missing in his life.

Except he couldn't for the life of him think of a flippant comment to make.

He turned away only to have Erica raise a questioning eyebrow at him from the other side of the kitchen, then glance meaningfully toward Avery. She was matchmaking! Erica had suspected his interest in Avery on the night of the oyster-and-champagne cocktail party, and it had become a certainty, he could read it on her face. Yet instead of irritation, Guy experienced a sudden unexpected bond with his half sister. And couldn't stop himself from winking at her.

Instantly Erica winked back.

"Okay, maybe it won't be so bad having another female in the family," said Guy with feigned reluctance.

"Good to know you feel that way." The sparkle in Erica's eyes outshone the radiance of the diamond solitaire on her ring finger.

Without intending to, Guy found himself seeking out Avery, and the approval in her sweet smile caused warmth to pool deep in his chest. For the first time since he'd come back to Jarrod Ridge he felt some degree of peace.

He had to remind himself that he wasn't the kind of man who indulged in emotion and soul-searching.

"The timer just went off," he said. "Which one of you three is going to cut me the first slice?"

Wearing her dressiest outfit the following night, a gold satin Versace dress that had been a gift from her aunt and uncle for her twenty-fifth birthday, Avery arrived early at the ballroom—more out of habit than anything else. She'd taken care with her makeup, and barely limped in the gold ballet flats she wore.

Camera crews were setting up for a segment that was to be filmed for a television show.

Guy was nowhere to be seen, and Avery rather suspected he was caught up in the kitchens overseeing the chefs, making sure that every detail was perfect. She was learning that the laid-back, carefree persona he cultivated concealed a far more complex, intense man. A perfectionist.

The wine selections had already been made—a collaboration between herself, Guy and Louis—and Avery was pleased with how well they complemented the dishes. Guy had been pleased, too.

She had done the job Uncle Art had wanted her to do. She would be leaving with her pride intact. Her heart was a different matter. There would be a large chunk left behind at Jarrod Ridge.

But she'd have Guy's baby to fill the hole.

Erica and a woman Avery had never seen before were fiddling with the flower arrangements.

"The flowers look beautiful," Avery told Guy's half sister. She smiled, and for the first time Avery saw a hint of Guy in her features. Her heart tugged. Would their baby have that look, too?

"Don't they?" Erica introduced Avery to the woman

standing beside her, a local florist, who was overjoyed to have been given the job for the fundraiser.

"I only opened my shop three months ago, this is an amazing break for my business."

"Avery is right, the arrangements do look beautiful. I'm sure you'll get a lot of business." Undetected, Guy had come up behind them. "Erica said from the start that you are very artistic."

"Christian and I will be among those customers—for our wedding. And heaven knows I'm not easily impressed." But Erica looked delighted with Guy's praise. "I'm so glad we're supporting local businesses."

"It was a great initiative."

Avery saw the glances Guy and Erica exchanged. There was understanding…and fondness. She couldn't help feeling pleased for Guy. The discovery of Erica's existence had been a shock—but both of them had gained so much.

The ballroom started to fill.

By the silver flashes of light Avery gathered that the beautiful group moving to one of the tables at the foot of the stage must be movie stars.

Gavin and Trevor came over to join them, both tanned and athletically built, with an appealing surf-and-sun openness that made them look so similar. Avery looked from one to the other, then to Blake and Guy. All four brothers were clad in tuxedos and looked devastatingly handsome. But only one held her heart….

"You know," she announced, "Gavin and Trevor should be twins. They look far more alike."

Erica was the first to agree. "Funny, I had a similar thought when I first arrived in Aspen."

"Let's go settle down at our table," Guy murmured to Avery.

The siblings had divided themselves among different

tables, to spread the effect of having hosts throughout the ballroom. Avery hadn't inspected the final table lists, but it made sense for her to sit with Guy. After all, they were working together, and it would be downright weird if she objected.

And her only reason to object was one she didn't want made public: she loved a man who didn't love her, and she was expecting his baby.

He rested his hand under her elbow, and the contact sent a shiver of awareness through Avery. Oh, heavens, would this wretched wanting ever stop?

It grew worse when she discovered that she had been seated beside him. His thigh brushed hers as he sat down, and she was conscious of his dinner-jacketed arm beside her bare arm. She shifted a little away—the seat on her other side was the only one at the table not yet occupied. To her surprise she found a familiar face on the other side of the empty seat.

It broke the ice.

"Nancy!" She turned her head. "Guy, this is Nancy who rescued me…and called you." When the excitement settled, Nancy introduced the older couple beside her as her parents.

"We've been coming to this event for years," said Nancy's mother. "But this is only the second time Nancy's been with us."

"I've been working in Boston." Nancy rested her fingers on her mother's arm. "But I decided I missed home. So I came back to Aspen."

"I'm back after years, too—" At the arrival of the white-jacketed waiter, Guy broke off.

Avery chose a spinach-and-bacon salad as a starter, while Guy had wild mushrooms. The wines she'd selected worked well as an accompaniment and she couldn't stop herself from giving Guy a triumphant smile as he kissed his fingertips in appreciation.

He leaned toward her. "We make a good team."

"Glad you've got confidence in me."

"I have every confidence in you."

"You didn't to start with." She tossed her head and gave him a mischievous smile. "Are you ready to eat your words?"

Then she froze.

Beyond Guy a man was wending his way through the tables, a man she'd hoped never to see again. Avery whispered, "What's he doing here?"

A desperate look around showed that the only empty seat was the one right beside her.

Guy glanced up as the newcomer stopped beside their table, and cursed.

Thirteen

"What are you doing here, Jeff?" Guy demanded.

Jeff stuck his hands in his pockets and swaggered forward. "Already forgotten that you ordered me to come?"

Avery gasped.

Guy placed a steadying hand on Avery's arm and felt her tremble.

"I arranged our meeting for Monday afternoon—not tonight." A fierce emotion filled Guy. Jeff had come to cause trouble. Guy didn't doubt it.

Jeff had tried to pressure her to sleep with him, and Guy no longer had any choice but to break his partnership with Jeff, and walk away from the years of friendship they'd shared.

He believed Avery trusted that she'd told him the truth.

Avery came first.

Stunned, Guy looked at her. He took in the doll-like features, the blue eyes, the tendrils of blond hair that had escaped her upswept hairstyle. Why had he never realized how important she'd become to him?

Because he hadn't wanted any commitment.

Hadn't wanted the pain—the loss and loneliness—it might bring. Yet when Avery departed for California there would be a chasm in his heart that no one else would be able to fill.

The empty feeling had a name. Grief. He was already missing Avery. But this was different to his father's experience. His father hadn't had a choice in losing his Mom.

He did.

And he wasn't going to let Avery go.

Or the baby.

They were his…and he was going to keep them both safe. In any way he could. It was about far more than sex, about sating his senses with her. It was about waking with her beside him in the morning, sharing a joke with her. Simply knowing she was in the same room as him brought him joy. That could only be love.

He loved her.

He narrowed his gaze on his business partner.

Jeff glared back.

"You shouldn't have come tonight, Jeff," he said quietly. "I would've listened to your side of the story on Monday."

Avery clambered to her feet. "Excuse me, I need the bathroom."

Guy gave her a few seconds to get a head start. Then turning to Jeff, he said, "Maybe you're right. Let's talk now and finish it. Come."

Without a second look, Guy rose to his feet leaving his erstwhile friend to follow.

Avery was standing in the pre-function lobby off the ballroom. In the light of the chandeliers overhead, Guy could see that her face was pinched with strain. Placing his hand around Jeff's arm, Guy marched Jeff over to where she stood.

Her blue eyes went wide.

"Jeff, first, I think you owe Avery an apology," Guy said as they reached her.

Avery's lips parted in astonishment.

"I have nothing to apologize for," Jeff blustered. "She got what she was asking for."

Avery started to object, but Guy was too quick. He stepped forward until he stood nose to nose with his business partner. "Then why have you all but disappeared off the face of the earth since I tried to call you to confront you with what Avery told me? Why did it take an e-mail from me saying that our business partnership was over before you had Vivienne contact me to set up a meeting for Monday?"

Beside him, Avery gasped.

"She lied to you," said Jeff heatedly.

"I haven't even told you what she accused you of, so how can you know that she lied?" Guy asked gently.

Jeff pulled a handkerchief from his pocket and wiped the beads of sweat that had popped out over his forehead.

"You're not going to let a little bitch like her ruin what we've built up together?"

"Watch yourself!" Guy's tone was as dangerous as a lash. "And she didn't ruin anything. You did that all by yourself."

"You don't really mean to dissolve our partnership." The bluster had evaporated.

Avery's hand touched his sleeve. "Guy, you don't have to—"

"You don't need her." Jeff spoke right over Avery. "Surely you don't intend to be ruled by a piece of—"

"Don't say it." Even Jeff knew better than to argue with the lethal softness.

Guy rested his hand on Avery's waist and drew her close.

"We're both waiting for your apology, Jeff."

Jeff looked from Avery to Guy and his shoulders sagged. "I'm sorry."

Avery tipped her head up. "He told you he didn't—"

"No," Guy cut across Avery's words. "He didn't have to. I know you told me the truth when you said that he arrived at my apartment pretending that I'd asked him to pick you up, and fed you a pack of lies. You need to believe that I never sent Jeff to you as a birthday gift. I had something else planned."

A flicker of curiosity lit her eyes, and she opened her mouth to say something. But Jeff spoke first, "I'd been drinking. Sometimes I do really stupid things when I drink."

Guy remembered that years ago when he'd first met Jeff he'd sometimes gotten into sticky situations at parties. It had stopped soon after. He'd thought Jeff had simply grown up. He'd never suspected that Jeff had a problem.

"But why lie to me?"

"I made a move on Avery, and I knew that if she told you, you would get rid of your share in Go Green. I never intended for that to happen."

Guy gave a laugh of disbelief. His fingers itched to yank Jeff by the collar and shake him like a dog. Avery would not appreciate such violence. "That's it?" he asked. "That's all you can come up with?"

"I'm sorry." Jeff seemed to shrink still further. "Give me another chance. You can't end our partnership. I'll resume the counseling I gave up a few years ago."

"I'm glad to hear that, Jeff," said Avery. "You need help."

"Our business relationship is over," said Guy.

Jeff looked utterly miserable. "You don't need to dissolve the partnership—I'll agree to it. I'll sell out my share."

"That's certainly an option for us to discuss Monday afternoon. But I can't talk now, I have some things I need to say to Avery first."

"I don't think I should come back into the ballroom—I've lost my appetite. I'll find a hotel in town."

"Just stay out of the resort bars," Guy said.

"Here," Jeff passed him an envelope. "It's a contribution to the fundraiser."

Guy nodded. The friendship he'd shared for years with Jeff would never recover from his deception but the man faced a tough road to rehabilitation. Guy had stared down enough of his own demons since his father's death, to know he wouldn't want to be in Jeff's shoes. And, if he played his cards right, he'd get to keep Avery. He could afford to be generous. "Thank you. I'll see you Monday, we'll deal with Go Green then."

Jeff shook the hand he'd offered. "I'll understand if you don't invite me to the wedding."

"There isn't going to be a wedding—so you won't miss anything." Avery said from beside him, then walked away.

A sense of helplessness filled Guy. What the hell was he supposed to do now?

There wouldn't be a wedding—they both knew that. Avery had never expected it—hell, she'd even told him that.

Avery settled herself down in the seat that had been intended for Jeff, so that the chair she'd been sitting on before created a no-man's-land between her seat and Guy's. She needed that dividing space right now.

Pushing her untouched plate away, she turned to Nancy and started to chatter about the coming ski season.

Inside she was seething.

How dare Guy tell Jeff that he loved her? Pretending he'd never doubted her, and that he'd accepted her word? Then without missing a beat, shaking the man's hand? She'd half expected him to slap Jeff jovially on the back.

Men. Avery had stifled the urge to yell at Guy like a fishwife. To be honest, she'd wanted him to floor Jeff.

"Avery, we need to talk."

She'd been so engrossed in her murderous thoughts she hadn't heard him come up behind her. To buy herself time before responding, she leaned sideways and reached for her half-full wine glass and took a long sip of the apple juice it contained to fortify her for the "talk" he wanted.

He slid into the vacant seat beside her, the seat she'd deliberately left open. Putting his arm around on the chair back behind her, he leaned forward.

"I wish I could've spared you that unpleasantness."

Before she could respond Erica was beside them. "Sorry to interrupt…Guy you should be up on the stage. The bidding is about to begin. Have you forgotten you pledged to prepare a meal for two?"

He turned his head to his half sister. "Give me one minute."

"There isn't time," Erica protested. "Not now."

Guy raked his hand through his hair and gave an impatient sigh. "Okay." The blowtorch force of his gaze landed on Avery. "And don't even think of running out on me again. Do you understand?"

She nodded, still furious, but glad that she'd been spared a public confrontation.

Guy followed Erica onto the stage.

Avery still couldn't believe Guy had shaken that jerk's hand. She was glad he was gone.

The first item to be auctioned off was a case of French

red that went for a staggering sum of money. A weekend in one of the private, fully staffed, Jarrod Ridge lodges with a balloon ride and other trimmings went next.

Guy was up a few minutes later.

Back in New York Guy had promised to prepare her a feast in person. It had never come to pass. And now it never would. But a couple of complete strangers would enjoy his ministrations.

Gathering up her bag, Avery said goodbye to Nancy and her parents, and pushed her chair back. Skirting the edge of the ballroom she left the glamorous event.

She couldn't bear to watch.

The Sky Lounge was deserted.

For the baby's sake, Avery ordered a cup of hot chocolate rather than coffee or tea and retreated to a high-backed armchair in the corner by the floor-to-ceiling window. Kicking the ballet flats off, she tucked her feet beneath her, taking care not to put too much weight on her ankle, and stared out through the glass at the pinpricks of lights that twinkled in the darkness outside.

The day after tomorrow she would be gone.

She placed a hand on her stomach.

"Then it will be just you and me, baby," she whispered.

A picture of Guy as he'd looked on stage, debonair in a his perfectly fitted tuxedo filled her mind. That was how she would forever remember him. The bartender set her chocolate down on the round table in front of the armchair and Avery smiled her thanks as she picked it up.

Fleetingly she wondered how much Guy's donation had sold for. Cradling the mug in her hands, she pictured the lucky anonymous couple he would entertain and feed.

Avery grew still.

Was that it? Was it easier for Guy to cook for complete strangers than for a lover? Cooking for a lover implied caring. Guy didn't do caring—it smacked too much of commitment. She'd fallen for a man who was as far removed from her family dream as it was possible to get.

Then she remembered his over-the-top concern for her at the hospital.

That hadn't been the reaction of a carefree, commitment-fearing man.

Some men fuss when they're worried.

She stared thoughtfully at the frothy cream on the top of the hot drink. Even the receptionist in the doctor's rooms had noticed Guy's concern about her. And his every action since had shown his concern and caring.

Why?

Thank God you're safe.

That's what he'd said to her after he'd climbed in behind her in the spa and held her like he never intended to let her go. Avery took a sip of the drink, barely tasting it. Was it possible that Guy really did love her? He'd told Jeff he did but she'd been too angry to take it in.

Yet he'd never told her.

Perhaps he was one of those men who couldn't talk about love. Her head drooped. Then she rallied. It wouldn't be the same as the love she felt for him…but it was a start. She could work on it.

Like the shifting of the brightly hued splinters of a kaleidoscope the fragments of a new vision were forming.

Had Guy been irrationally afraid she might die?

His mother had died…

In the same hospital? Could it be that he'd envisaged his worst childhood nightmare recurring?

He'd never had a chance to say goodbye to his mother….

And she'd walked away from him in New York without saying goodbye.

What had he said just before he'd gone up on stage with Erica? *And don't even think of running out on me again. Do you understand?* And what had she done? She'd promptly walked out and retreated here to the Sky Lounge.

She'd left.

Again.

Horror filled her. Guy would believe she didn't care. If Guy truly loved her that would hurt, maybe cause him to withdraw behind the lighthearted mask that she was starting to detest.

Hastily she slipped her shoes back on and rose to her feet, only to stop in her tracks at the sight of Guy coming toward her.

The expression of apprehension on Avery's face caused Guy to rethink his plan of sweeping her off her feet and carrying her to his suite so they could have uninterrupted time for the talk he was determined to have with her.

Then he threw caution to the winds. He beckoned. "You're coming with me."

To his surprise, instead of arguing, Avery trotted over to him as quietly as a lamb.

"I shouldn't have left." The words bubbled from her. "I told you I was staying—then I didn't."

Guy shot her a puzzled look, but capitalized on her momentary meekness by grasping her hand in his. Her fingers tightened around his own.

"To hell with it."

She squeaked as he lifted her high into his arms, and strode out of the Sky Lounge ignoring the stunned expression of the bar staff.

It didn't take them long to reach the elevator to the private suites, and once inside the silence was electric. Guy gazed into her eyes. "We are going to talk."

"Yes."

"And you are going nowhere."

She nodded.

"You're not leaving, understand?"

"Yes, Guy."

"Good," he purred hoping that this unaccustomed subservience would last a little longer.

When the car came to a stop, he exited with Avery held high against his chest. Once through the hallway, he turned left and marched past the arched windows that looked out onto the starlit sky.

When he halted outside his suite, he said, "The access card is in my pocket." Then steeled himself as her fingers fumbled in his dinner jacket. Avery swiped it in the key slot, then he pushed the door open. Once inside the suite he closed the door, and let her slide down his body, before he leaned back against the heavy wooden door.

Avery narrowed the Barbie-blue eyes that had tied him up in knots. "Are you going to stand there all night long? Because it doesn't look terribly comfortable."

"I'm making sure you don't run out on me. Tonight you're staying with me all night long."

He heard her breath catch.

Then she said gently, "You don't need to worry. I have no intention of going anywhere."

The stiffness in his clenched jaw eased a little, and he stepped away from the door.

"I only have one demand," she said as she sank down on the sofa.

"What is that?"

"That you promise to trust me for as long as we are together."

"I trust you," Guy said with the solemnity of a vow. He knelt at her feet and picked up her left hand. "And I hate to admit it, but you were right when you taunted me about being jealous. I was jealous. But only because you are the only woman it hurt me to lose. I didn't know what had hit me."

"You didn't react when I said that Louis should take me on the picnic," she pointed out.

"Your mockery made me realize how much of an idiot I'd become. I didn't know what was happening to me. You're a terrifying little thing, you know."

She gave a gurgle of laughter. "Little things can't be terrifying."

"You are. You scared me to death," he confessed.

Avery leaned forward until the tip of her nose almost touched his. "You don't need to be jealous—there is only you, and I'm not going anywhere."

"Damn right you're not going anywhere," he growled. "At least, not without me."

"Then I'll stay."

"That will be forever. I want—"

"Guy—" she placed a finger against his lips "—you don't need to promise me forever. We'll take it one day at a time."

"But I want forever." He bent his head and placed a kiss on the ring finger. "Tomorrow we will go shopping for a ring."

"Guy!" Avery started to laugh. "You can't just tell me that. You need to ask me to marry you first. It's called a proposal."

He sat back on his heels and looked up at her, and shook his head. "I'm not taking any chance that you might say no."

Stretching out a hand, Avery stroked the engaging lock

that had fallen over his forehead back in to place. "I would never say no, trust me on that."

He drew a deep, shuddering breath. "I trust you with my life. Avery, I'm sorry for having been such a dumb idiot. I'll never doubt you again. Please marry me."

"Why?"

Here it was. She wanted blood. She deserved it. He shut his eyes. To his shock her lips touched his, and his eyes shot open. The butterfly kiss ended, and then she murmured, "I know I want to marry you because I love you."

Guy blinked at her. "Promise?"

"I promise."

"I love you, too," he said in a rush. Then he gave a shaky laugh. "That wasn't as hard as I thought it would be."

"It will get easier—and that's a promise too." She wrinkled her nose at him.

Linking his fingers behind her neck, Guy gazed deep into her eyes, enthralled by the understanding, the love, the devotion he glimpsed there. "I love you, Avery Lancaster-soon-to-be-Jarrod. I've fought it, I've distrusted my feelings, I've done and said some incredibly stupid things. But you have to believe I want you to be my wife. I want our baby… and whatever other babies might be in the future for us. I want us to be a family."

The smile she gave him was blinding.

"Sometimes dreams do come true," she whispered and leaned forward.

Guy met her half way. The kiss was hungry. Passionate. Perfect.

"I think it's time we went to bed," said Avery with a delicious smile.

Pale gold light from the bedside lamp broke the pre-dawn darkness in the bedroom. Avery pressed a button on her cell phone ending the call and set the slim phone down on the bed stand.

"Wake up," she urged the man sprawled on his stomach, his hand still resting on her thigh.

Guy groaned and cracked open an eye. "Good Lord, it's still night."

"Come, there's something we've got to do."

"At this hour? What?"

Avery gave him an impish grin as she clambered out of bed. "You'll see."

When they got down to the lobby fifteen minutes later, he stopped dead at the sight of the huddle of strangers in the lobby. "What is this?"

"We're going ballooning."

"No." Panic flared in his eyes.

"Hey, what's wrong? I thought this was what you wanted. You've been telling me I need to take more risks."

"I've changed my mind." His voice was muffled.

"Guy," Avery hooked her arms around his shoulders and drew his head down to look into his dark eyes. "What's wrong?"

"I don't want to lose you." His lips barely moved.

"You won't lose me."

"I have once—through my own stupidity when I didn't come after you and allowed you to go back to California. In the past few days I nearly lost you again—" he shuddered "—the car accident. I don't want you taking any risks."

"Well, you can hardly wrap me in cotton wool for the rest of my life," she said reasonably.

"I can damn well try."

"Too late." Avery wove her fingers through his and tugged. "It's all organized. We've got our own balloon and our own pilot."

"I must've been mad to suggest this," he muttered.

"Insane," she said cheerfully, "but you assured me it was safer than driving, remember? And you said it was a great way to see bears."

Guy groaned.

Within half an hour they were ready to ascend. The gas burner roared and the yellow envelope of the balloon was swollen and round. The first rays of the sun caressed Avery's uptilted face, giving it a radiance Guy had never seen.

She was exquisite.

And she was his.

"What about if I cook you a meal instead?" he asked with final desperation. "Whatever you want, you choose."

She met his eyes. Hers were sparkling with excitement. "What did you say? I'm looking forward to this. A little while ago I was dreading it, now I simply can't wait."

Damn, she hadn't even heard his final plea and he couldn't deprive her of the pleasure of the experience of a lifetime. Guy stopped fighting and took her hand in his.

"Stand beside me," she said, turning away to scan the valley below the resort, "I want you to feel exactly what I do."

Hell. His stomach churned. He didn't even want to think of her fear of heights. Instead he enfolded her in his arms from behind and crossed his hands over her belly. In his arms Avery—and his baby—would be safe.

The basket heaved and rose off the ground. Avery let out a whoop. The ascent went perfectly. Soon they were gliding over a grove of aspens.

Avery stuck her hand out and her fingers touched the topmost leaves.

"Come back here." Guy hauled her against his chest.

She turned into his arms so that she was facing him and

grinned at him. "I can't believe how fantastic this is. It's so smooth—despite the noise of the gas."

Resisting the urge to say "I told you so," he kissed the tip of her nose. "I'm glad you're having a good time." And he was.

"Well, I decided if you could overcome your fear of loving someone and admit you loved me, then it should be easy for me to overcome my fear of heights."

Her admission tightened his throat. "Avery—"

"Before you say I didn't have to do it, believe me I did. And it might've started off being for you. But now it's all for me. I feel utterly free—and it's not because I'm in the place I always considered to be the realm of angels." She gestured to the sky above them.

"It's been liberating for me, too," admitted Guy.

The sense of freedom was exhilarating. The burdens that had been pressing on him for years, the fear of commitment, the need to prove himself, had all lifted. Everything that mattered in his world was contained in the circle of his arms.

"I love you, Avery." This time the words came easily, as she'd promised. "And before I forget, I've got a date tonight."

She arched an eyebrow. "With me I hope?"

"With the winner of my auction donation."

"Oh." For a moment her eyes clouded over then cleared, and the blue eclipsed the cobalt sky above them. "I'll see you afterward."

"Don't you want to know who placed the winning bid?"

"Who?"

"I did."

Her eyes widened. "You did? But why pay for yourself?"

"We have unfinished business." At her puzzlement, he

added, "I have a birthday dinner to prepare for you. You missed out last time."

"That's what you were doing that night?"

He nodded. "I'd prepared you dinner at Baratin. But tonight will be better. Because as soon as we land we're going to go shopping for a ring. And later I'll place it here." He stroked her ring finger.

"We'll also need to tell your family about our engagement."

"They'll be delighted." Guy grinned as he imagined what Erica would have to say. "And tomorrow I'll fly to California with you to break the news to your family, too. Then we'll come back home."

Jarrod Ridge was home, would always be his home, Guy knew.

"There's a meadow beyond Willow Lodge overlooking Roaring Fork that I want you to see. If you like it we can build a home there."

"It sounds perfect." She gave him a gentle smile. "I'd like to keep the news about the baby to ourselves for now. It's so new, I want a bit of time for us to savor it alone. Is that selfish?"

"Not at all. The baby will be our secret," Guy said and he stroked her stomach, which still showed no sign of the life, the part of him and Avery that was growing inside. "The announcement will make a wonderful Christmas present for both our families."

"And in the meantime," her voice dropped to a breathy drawl that had Guy lowering his head to hear what she was saying, "we'll have plenty of nights to spend together."

Together. To Guy that sounded like heaven.

* * * * *

COMING NEXT MONTH

Available September 14, 2010

#2035 WHAT A WESTMORELAND WANTS
Brenda Jackson
Man of the Month

#2036 EXPECTING THE RANCHER'S HEIR
Kathie DeNosky
Dynasties: The Jarrods

#2037 DANTE'S TEMPORARY FIANCÉE
Day Leclaire
The Dante Legacy

#2038 STAND-IN BRIDE'S SEDUCTION
Yvonne Lindsay
Wed at any Price

#2039 AT THE BILLIONAIRE'S BECK AND CALL?
Rachel Bailey

#2040 THE SECRET CHILD & THE COWBOY CEO
Janice Maynard

HARLEQUIN®

A *Romance*

FOR EVERY MOOD™

Spotlight on

Heart & Home

Heartwarming romances
where love can happen
right when you least expect it.

See the next page to enjoy a sneak peek
from Harlequin Superromance®,
a Heart and Home series.

*Enjoy a sneak peek at fan favorite Molly O'Keefe's
Harlequin Superromance miniseries,*
THE NOTORIOUS O'NEILLS, *with*
TYLER O'NEILL'S REDEMPTION,
*available September 2010
only from Harlequin Superromance.*

Police chief Juliette Tremblant recognized the shape of the man strolling down the street—in as calm and leisurely fashion as if it were the middle of the day rather than midnight. She slowed her car, convinced her eyes were playing tricks on her. It had been a long time since Tyler O'Neill had been seen in this town.

As she pulled to a stop at the curb, he turned toward her, and her heart about stopped.

"What the hell are you doing here, Tyler?"

"Well, if it isn't Juliette Tremblant." He made his way over to her, then leaned down so he could look her in the eye. He was close enough to touch.

Juliette was not, repeat, *not* going to touch Tyler O'Neill. Not with her fingers. Not with a ten-foot pole. There would be no touching. Which was too bad, since it was the only way she was ever going to convince herself the man standing in front of her—as rumpled and heart-stoppingly handsome now as he'd been at sixteen—was real.

And not a figment of all her furious revenge dreams.

"What are you doing back in Bonne Terre?" she asked.

"The manor is sitting empty," Tyler said and shrugged, as though his arriving out of the blue after ten years was casual. "Seems like someone should be watching over the family home."

"You?" She laughed at the very notion of him being here for any unselfish reason. "Please."

He stared at her for a second, then smiled. Her heart fluttered against her chest—a small mechanical bird powered by that smile.

"You're right." But that cryptic comment was all he offered.

Juliette bit her lip against the other questions.

Why did you go?

Why didn't you write? Call?

What did I do?

But what would be the point? Ten years of silence were all the answer she really needed.

She had sworn off feeling anything for this man long ago. Yet one look at him and all the old hurt and rage resurfaced as though they'd been waiting for the chance. That made her mad.

She put the car in gear, determined not to waste another minute thinking about Tyler O'Neill. "Have a good night, Tyler," she said, liking all the cool "go screw yourself" she managed to fit into those words.

It seems Juliette has an old score to settle with Tyler.
Pick up TYLER O'NEILL'S REDEMPTION
to see how he makes it up to her.
Available September 2010,
only from Harlequin Superromance.

MARGARET WAY

introduces

THE *Rylance* DYNASTY

**The lives & loves of
Australia's most powerful family**

Growing up in the spotlight hasn't been easy, but the two
Rylance heirs, Corin and his sister, Zara, have come of age
and are ready to claim their inheritance. Though they are
privileged, proud and powerful, they are about to discover
that there are some things money can't buy....

Look for:
Australia's Most Eligible Bachelor
Available September

Cattle Baron Needs a Bride
Available October

Silhouette Desire

New York Times and *USA TODAY*
bestselling author

BRENDA JACKSON

brings you

WHAT A WESTMORELAND WANTS,

another seductive Westmoreland tale.

MAN of the MONTH

Part of the Man of the Month series

Callum is hopeful that once he gets
Gemma Westmoreland on his native turf
he will wine and dine her with a seduction plan
he has been working on for years—one that
guarantees to make her his.

Available September wherever books are sold.

**Look for a new Man of the Month
by other top selling authors each month.**

Always Powerful, Passionate and Provocative.